# TOXINS
## (AND OTHER POISONS)

Silvia Romano

*to Ilaria,*
*and to the Love*

**TOXINS (AND OTHER POISONS)**
Silvia Romano

ISBN 978-1903110775

First published in this edition 2021 by Wrecking Ball Press

Copyright © Silvia Romano

Book design: humandesign.co.uk

Supported using public funding by
ARTS COUNCIL
ENGLAND
LOTTERY FUNDED

# CONTENT

# TOOTHACHE

At exactly ten to eight on a Thursday evening, Mr. Tannenbaum, just after taking his first bite of his steak, felt, while chewing, a bothersome pain on the left side of the floor of his mouth. His wife shot him a concerned glance from the other end of the table.

"You should really go to the dentist."

Her husband had been postponing a dental appointment for months, excusing himself because of work-related or personal reasons.

The dentist's waiting room glared with neon lights reflected in the dopey eyes of the fish swimming lazily in the aquarium.

Mr. T was welcomed by a cacophony of coughs and glaring eyes. A man wearing a hat and a turquoise scarf browsed through the pages of a rumpled magazine, making a dry sound, like dead leaves. After an eternal wait, Tannenbaum was directed by a secretary into a pod-like white office, where she placed a bib on him, leaving him to contemplate the several sinister, hooked and shiny tools, sprawled out side-by-side on a cloth.

"How's it going, Mr. T? We haven't seen each other in a long time, the last time I think I still had all of my hair!" boomed the dentist, placing his hands on either side of his tray of torture devices.

"Not bad...it's just this tooth, it bothers me a little," Tannenbaum said, pointing at the offending spot with his finger.

"Let's have a look."

With a forceful push from the dentist, the automatic chair sent Mr. T belly-up. He opened up nice and wide so the dentist could scrutinise his oral cavity with a mirror.

The dentist noticed immediately that near the cavity on the right-side bottom molar there was something out of the ordinary, and he abandoned his mirror in favor of a handheld microscope with a wide-angle lens. Focusing, he detected a rather uncommon scenario: on the tooth enamel, the intense activity of a swarm of small beings who busied themselves in a series of actions.

The dentist straightened up, astounded.

"Mr. T...it's baffling! It seems that in the cavity that has formed in your molar, some microorganisms are building a community!"

Mr. T was beyond surprised.

"A town? In my tooth?"

"There's no doubt." the dentist replied "and they seem to be properly organised as well! I see they have already erected a Town Hall. That one must be the mayor. And there are the council members. I wish you could see it yourself! I'd have you get an X-Ray, if I weren't afraid that it would cause irreversible damage to this civilisation."

He fumbled a little more with the lenses.

"Yes, that's it. The pain you're feeling is caused by the construction of a hospital for lepers. Oh! Would you look at that! There's an unfortunate soul inching along in a wheelchair! Poor devil."

Mr. Tannenbaum had the feeling of being trapped in a scorching moral dilemma. He prided himself on being a zealous advocate of democracy and free speech. He never would have thought that one day he would have discovered himself to be what the asteroid had been for the dinosaurs, or the colonists for the Native Americans: in other words, to hold the power to wipe out a blooming civilisation. In mutual agreement with the dentist, he decided it was worth it to endure the pain for the greater good, not to act in haste and to get a prescription for paracetamol. Every week, he selflessly sacrificed himself laying on the dentist's chair to monitor the progress of that unexpected event, and every week it seemed the community was making progress in its development; here representatives of the people were elected; there a new elementary school was opened. Mr. T started to think about his little republic with affection. He was mindful to chew with the other side of his mouth and not to use toothpaste directly on the tooth, but just around it. He felt deeply guilty when, flossing, he caused the collapse of a bridge, with the consequent death of seven workers.

One Monday, the dentist looked up from his molar, puzzled. Over the last few days, the pain of decayed tooth hammered with more insistence than usual, and even the painkillers had started to lose their effectiveness.

"It looks like they have formed a trade union."

"A trade union?" astonished an amused Mr. T.

"Yes. It seems that, after the bridge event, the citizens don't feel safe anymore. They organised a sit-in with flags and banners, for occupational safety and health, and they are stationed outside the town hall."

"Seriously?" laughed T, indulgently.

That evening, he took a double ration of his medicine and entirely avoided cleaning the right side of his mouth in order to prevent further calamities.

A week of dead calmness followed.

"They are currently on strike," reported the dentist, taking his eye away from the microscope. "The price of bread has increased, and discontent is spreading. The people don't feel safe anymore. A speech is now taking place at union headquarters."

Suddenly, speaking in a confidential tone, he said, "But it's a secret meeting. Rumour has it, the citizens want to remove the mayor. They think he is not capable of governing. One member of the organising committee is running for leadership of the new popular revolutionary movement. It looks like he's gaining a lot of support."

That evening, Mr. T brushed his teeth on tiptoes.

A couple of nights later, his sleep was interrupted by a brutal electric shock that made him jump out of bed in pain. The dentist was urgently summoned, he arrived quickly still wearing his pajamas and carrying his wide-angle lens.

"We're dealing with an attack" he explained, after ogling what was going on in there. "The pain is provoked by the effect of paper bombs being lit off. Things are moving very fast. After the strike, the citizens have taken the hard line. They voted for the impeachment of the mayor and the popular party leader is now the new representative in parliament."

The dentist left, promising to check in again as soon as possible and left a prescription for a strong sedative.

Once the doctor left, Mr. T's wife pleaded with her husband to reconsider his point of view, to intervene and wipe the slate clean with a filling. She had witnessed the entire scene from the door, wrapped in her gown, a worried look on her face.

"This is going too far, Gerald. You did what you could, but it's all fun and games until someone loses an eye."

*Or a tooth*, Mr. Tannenbaum thought.

But he refused to play the role of dictator. He had a violent argument with his wife over the right to protest and freedom of the press, he ended up sleeping on the couch. A week later all hell broke loose. The dentist had started to look more hesitant and alarmed at every new appointment. The new leader had organised a trained militia and kept giving speeches that progressively grew more radical: he talked about rebellion and fighting the enemy, he showed the desire to conquer neighbouring territories, claiming benefits of common concern. The people supported him; frequently, dumpsters were set on fire, leaving Mr. T with a burnt taste in his mouth. It got to a point where even the dentist made it clear that carrying on like they were could create irreversible damage, but Mr. T was unyielding. He alleged that popular sovereignty was the cornerstone of democracy, and he categorically refused to suffocate the freedom of speech.

One day the dentist looked at him with a serious face, causing him inner turmoil. He had felt an odd weakness for days now, the toothache was by now a constant presence, and he felt feverish.

"Mr. T, things have gotten out of hand. The situation is no longer under our control. The revolt has reached the root."

"Okay," surrendered Mr. T, with a hint of nervousness in his voice. "I authorise you to use the drill."

The dentist shook his head, mournfully.

"There's nothing you can do. You have permanently lost your tooth."

"All right," insisted Mr. T, the hint of nervousness starting grow. "Pull it, then. We'll eradicate the problem entirely. The hole will remain, but that's fine. I'll wear an implant."

"You don't understand," said the dentist in a tone of voice that frightened him "the matter is now beyond my competence. The tooth decay has turned into an abscess. It needs to be removed, and I can't do it in the clinic. I suggest you go immediately to a surgeon for the intervention."

Mr. T promptly rushed to the nearest ER, where his blood was drawn and analysed. The results showed that his platelet count was extremely low, the attending physician ordered an emergency CT scan of the lung. Mr. T was hooked to an IV, gripped by a delirious fever. The microorganisms that caused the untreated dental abscess had developed into septicemia.

Mr. Gerald Tannenbaum died on the operating table, during the attempt to save his lungs, eaten by the infection.

The mourners at the funeral said they were all amazed by the catastrophic result of a simple toothache.

# THE DEBT

Hank Bradshaw was not dreaming of anything, when he was suddenly awakened by the unmistakable noise of a metal object rolling near his front door.

He sat up dazed. The room was dark, but some light filtered in from beneath the closed shutters. It must have been morning. The sound of muffled voices and other unidentifiable noises were coming from the hallway.

Ever since living alone, Hank had gotten into the habit of lining up beer bottles and empty tinned cans in front of the front door before going to sleep. It was more of a placebo effect to help him sleep at night rather than an effective, preventative safety measure.

He rose from the worn-out mattress and crossed the hallway in a state of near sleepwalking, scratching his ass through a pair of loosened boxers. He was more disoriented, than nervous. It's easy to imagine his astonishment when opening the door, he found himself face-to-face with an unknown blonde woman who was standing in his doorway with her hands on her hips. She was surrounded by several boxes filled to the brim and two or three soft cotton bags piled up next to the door: it seemed like she was deciding where to start.

A boy of around seven years old stood near her, running his hands over the wallpaper, poking at the light switches, and every pre-existent element of furniture in the room.

For a moment, Hank believed that he was still sleeping. Then, the woman raised her eyes to him and, upon seeing him there, in undershirt and underpants in the doorway, let out a piercing shriek, which instantly snapped Hank out of his sleepy stupor.

"Who are you? What are you doing here?!" howled the stranger, pulling the boy behind her back.

"I live here," Hank replied, no less appalled. "Who are you, and how did you get in?"

From an adjacent room, a man promptly rushed in, lured by the call of the wild. He was stout and ruddy faced, his complexion gave him the appearance of a drunken lumberjack. Thinking Hank was a burglar, the man's eyes darted from left to right, searching for a weapon. For an instant, Hank feared the man would launch the child at him. Instead, the man angrily unscrewed one of the protruding hooks from the coat rack, the first blunt instrument he could lay his hands on.

Hank quickly raised his arms in surrender.

"What are you doing in my house?" the man snapped, clearly worked up.

"What are you talking about?" protested Hank. "This is my home. I've been living here for more than forty years, since the day I was born."

"There must be a misunderstanding," the woman butted in, trying to calm her hot-blooded companion while at the same time keeping the child safe behind her back. "They didn't tell us that...the thing is, the house has been assigned by the government to my husband and I. We have the keys. You see?"

Under his nose, she waved a bunch of keys held together by a snap-hook that Hank didn't recognise. "That's how we got in. It's our house, now. Richard, show the man the lease."

"I'm not showing him shit!" Richard snapped indignantly. "As far as I'm concerned, this man illegally broke into my apartment, and I want him to get the fuck out of here, now!"

"Richard!" his wife firmly scolded. Hank wondered if she was showing respect for him or if she didn't like profanities being used in front of the child. She turned to Hank with forced kindness.

"Are you sure you didn't receive an eviction order?"

"I haven't received any such notice. On the other hand, I don't see how any of this could be possible. I've always paid my rent and on time," murmured Hank, pointing at a wobbly cabinet by the door. "If you open that drawer, you'll find all the receipts. I paid this month's rent just last week."

The man was still sporting a belligerent look. Clearly, he didn't believe a word he was hearing, and he thought Hank was a vagrant. The woman, however, looked more willing to trust in his good faith.

"It certainly must be a misunderstanding," she said, in a more conciliatory tone. "Contact Housing Policies, at the State Office for Relocation and Collection. I am sure they will be able to settle the matter."

For the moment, it was clear that they had no intentions to leave.

Hank was compelled to put sweatpants on to cover his modesty and leave the battlefield without even washing his face. As soon as he crossed the threshold, the door was promptly shut behind his back. Hank felt as if a chapter of his life had been slammed shut right in his own face. Strangers were claiming rights to the very walls where he had spent his entire existence.

In his rush to leave, pursued by the man's gaze (which for a second hadn't ceased to follow him with a repulsed look, still holding the coat rack hook like a baseball bat) Hank had forgotten to take his own copy of the keys. He was now a prisoner outside his own home, and for no apparent reason.

The State Office of Relocation and Collection was a living hell like all other government departments. Hank's aversion towards bureaucracy, a distaste that may have been innate, had often led him to renounce taking advantage of the meagre benefits which people of the lowest rank, like him, were entitled to. The procedures to follow for obtaining such benefits were so complicated, that it just wasn't worth the hassle. The system was arranged as an organised chaos whereby if you were eligible for a crumb of assistance, they still wanted you to earn it. Mitchell from the factory said it was all designed to make people give up before receiving what was rightfully theirs. Hank's father had always told him that, in his humble opinion, what was his by right was still not enough compared to the torments he had to endure in the attempt of getting it; Hank was of the same opinion. The whole process included mountains of articles and commas; phrases written in such obscure legal mumbo jumbo that his simple mind was unable to decipher it. The provided electronic support services were of no use at all: the truth was that if you didn't know somebody who could pull strings in those departments, you could be left to die.

Hank avoided these offices like the plague. He had discovered the right strategy to get by in peace and tranquility, without too much damage: always do your duty, always pay what you owed, never ask for more than your fair share (even if, in theory, you were entitled to more); and, until then, he had never experienced any trouble at all.

The office was a beehive buzzing with busy individuals who bustled from one side to the other of the huge rooms, shuffling their feet on the linoleum floor. Men and women approached the counters and took their leave with the efficiency of a military exercise. Gigantic billboards displayed rows and rows of letters and numbers without providing any reasonable explanation as to what they meant.

Up front, he was greeted by a massive panel connected via wireless to a huge touch screen display that spat out different numbers related to different procedures through a tactile sensitivity system. Hank pressed his right hand on the number corresponding to ACCOMMODATION AND RESIDENCY and selected the number for TAX CHARGES with his left hand too, for safety. Each hand now had a label imprinted directly on his skin. Had he changed his mind, he wouldn't have known where to impress a third label. Pleased with his choices, Hank sat on one of the ugly plastic chairs scattered around, next to a buxom woman with a baby, whom he found adorable before it started a whiny, unjustified temper tantrum. Hank waited patiently for his turn. After a couple of geological eras, he felt his right hand heating up, and looking down at the label, he saw that "ACCOMMODATION AND RESIDENCY" was glowing, signaling that he was next. His turn was announced to the onlookers by an electrical buzzer. Hank stood up and walked to the counter, passing by a man wearing a hat and a turquoise scarf who was leaving, his hands in his pockets.

A woman was sitting behind a desk taller than Hank. Even though he wasn't a short man, he had to stand on his tiptoes to look her in the eye. She was the sort of woman unattainable to someone like Hank. Thin and flawless, not too much jewelry but just enough, smooth face, she was gracefully typing on a keyboard linked wirelessly to a hologram display, wrists wrapped in a tight pink blouse. When she detected his presence, she looked at him from behind a pair of small, gold-rimmed glasses.

"Yes?"

"My name's Hank. Hank Bradshaw," he started, with heavy breath. He noticed his slow pace was already starting to annoy her. "This morning I found strangers in my house."

The lady wiggled her nose.

"I think the competent authority you have to address in this case is the police," she said with a kind crocodile-like smile, readying her pretty finger to push the button for the next customer.

"No, wait, they weren't burglars," said Hank, "they had the keys, they received them from the government. My apartment has been assigned to them, but I still live there. They told me it may be some sort of mistake concerning a non-payment, or something like that. They suggested I come here."

She pulled her tapered fingers away from the button.

"We'll check right away," she declared, opening a virtual window in the air in front of her using the thumb and forefinger of her right hand, typing with the left one on the keyboard. "Can I have your electronic document?"

Hank gave her his ID and she diligently scanned it. On the hologram appeared the stored data of his whole life.

"Serial number 1208PQ, Hank B. born in A., only living son of S. and P. B., both deceased, right?"

"Right," confirmed Hank.

"Six foot, 200 pounds, clean bill of health. DNA sample, acquired. From which we infer the Employment Status, identified. Lowest range worker at the State Cement Factory."

"Precisely."

"Civil status, unmarried."

"There's someone," slipped out Hank, half-heartedly.

The lady shot him a skewed glance.

"But we're not really married." Hank dreamily thought of Rosie and her silky, midnight hair. "Not yet."

"So, no," concluded the lady, clicking on a key.

Hank remained seated with folded hands.

"Resident in a rental state-owned council house on 327 State Street, block 15 number 23?"

Hank nodded in the exact same moment that the impeccable lady warily raised an eyebrow.

"Uhm."

"Uhm...what?"

She raised her thin glasses from the screen.

"Mr. Bradshaw, the apartment has been impounded because you appear to be in default."

Hank almost fainted on the desk.

"In a...what?"

"It's listed as a delay in the payment of a bond," said the lady, perusing her screen with scrunched eyebrows. "A delay of over forty years... Mr. Bradshaw, you have never paid your Existence Tax!

"My what?" croaked Hank like a broken record.

She sighed and slowly took off her glasses.

"You are aware of the tax liability that takes effect at the moment of birth, right?"

"What are you talking about?"

"No one in your family has ever told you?"

"I don't have the slightest idea," confessed Hank, confused and dejected.

The impeccable lady opened a page on the holoscreen and scrolled it in front of him with a nonchalant motion of the thumb. The page danced before his nose. Clauses were marked in red on what looked like a contract densely written. There was his name on it, and numbers, numbers which amounted to a frightening total.

"At the moment of birth, parents need to go to the designated office in the district of residence and unlock the password for the Existence Tax form. Everyone receives it as soon as they are recorded in the civil registry. It's a user's daily maintenance charge due annually, until the time of death."

"User? User of what?"

The impeccable lady was sincerely astonished.

"Of what? Of the space you take up!" she cried out, shocked, "of the air you breathe!"

"A tax for living?" Hank was no less stunned. "That's crazy!"

Her eyes flashed with anger.

"You are the same as all other human beings, you are a person who uses and consumes precious resources. Perhaps you think that the planet and society can afford to host you for free?" she said, disgusted. "With your existence alone, you're stealing someone else's space. Why do you think you should be given special treatment?"

Hank, who had never in his life dared to believe he was more important than anyone else, stared at her, bewildered.

"I…"

"Your family never paid your tax," the lady cut in, "nor did you when you reached adulthood. If you don't proceed with the fulfillment of the debt by the end of the year, a surtax shall be applied."

"Surtax corresponding to…?" asked Hank, trembling.

"The tax-assessed value, tripled."

Hank closed his eyes.

"Mr. Bradshaw, you are a debtor. You have 2,500 years of debt to settle. The seizure of your apartment has been carried out to recoup part of the total amount of the debt. A very small amount, I have to say."

"I don't know what to say," panted Hank. "I've always lived in that apartment, since I was born, and we never received any notice."

"The leasing contract was registered to a third-party?" asked the impeccable lady.

"To my father."

"Freshly deceased?"

"Four weeks."

"When your father died, the system automatically assigned the house to you, since you're the heir. However, after a monthly check, the computer rescinded your lease on the apartment, because your debt with the government is so high, you were already in default. Your home has evidently been allotted to someone more deserving, against the sum you owe to the public treasury."

"My parents must not have known anything about this regulation - my father was just a labourer," murmured Hank, "and a good person. They both were good people. Honest people. They would have certainly paid what they owed."

"I am afraid one doesn't inherit only positive traits from one's parents, Mr. B," said the secretary, oozing severity. "Are you familiar with the saying 'the sins of the father fall on the children'?"

Hank held up his arms.

"Isn't there anything I can do to repay what I owe?"

The holoscreen slid away and the impeccable lady went back to typing on the keyboard with her fingers.

"I am sorry, what are you checking?"

"I am verifying what will happen if we withhold your monthly salary," she clarified. "How long would it take for you to extinguish the debt."

"You can't do that!" protested Hank, vehemently.

The impeccable lady's eyes snapped up like a chameleon.

"I mean, with all due respect," huffed Hank, his armpits moistening, "if you take away my salary, I'll have to eat from garbage cans. I am alone, and between rent and expenses, I barely make it to the end of the month as it is."

"It doesn't matter, it is not a feasible solution anyway," said the lady, briskly. "The system calculated that, at that rate, the debt would take over 500 years to be settled. Despite the wonders of science and technology, frankly Mr. Bradshaw, I doubt you will survive for such a long period of time. You have no heirs that can settle the account on your behalf, right?"

"No." said Hank, by now beaten.

The lady looked at him with a glance that one reserves for insects.

"You do understand, Mr. Bradshaw, that one way or another, this money must be paid. You have an open account with the State that increases day by day. A citizen is granted some services, but it is not right to take, take, take without giving anything back to society, that makes the efforts to support you, don't you think?"

"I...the thing is...surely..." babbled Hank, who, confronted with such a diversion from common sense, was left speechless.

"Not giving back that money, it's like you're stealing from the State every day, Mr. Bradshaw. It's like you're stealing from every one of us."

"Look," panted Hank, gripped by a sudden feeling of pride, "I've always worked, ever since I can remember, and I am not trying to take advantage by any means. I had no idea of the existence of this tax - nobody in my family ever told me. Otherwise, I would have found a way to pay it years ago!"

The impeccable lady raised a highfalutin eyebrow.

"Listen, I just want to get my debt in order," persevered Hank. "You tell me how to do it. I don't have a house anymore; I don't have a car. I have nothing."

She drummed with her fingers on the desk, scratching her nails over the lacquered surface.

"Mr. Bradshaw, I won't lie to you. Your situation can be defined as desperate. Nevertheless, I have faith that with your collaboration we will be able to find a solution."

"Anything," Hank replied frantically, leaning into his hands on the tabletop.

After a brief pause, interspersed by the typing of the keys, the lady raised her gaze from the holoscreen.

"At this point, all that remains for me to suggest, is a contribution through the only thing that in your current state you are able to offer, Mr. Bradshaw."

"And what would that be?"

"Your time."

"My time?" repeated Hank like a parrot, confusedly.

"It's the only option I have left to propose in your case, Mr. Bradshaw," said the impeccable lady. "That, fundamentally, is the only property you own."

"And how do I do that?" asked Hank, appalled.

"It's very simple," she explained with a sigh. "We're talking about the transfer of your non-operative time, the one we vulgarly refer to as 'free time'."

She leaned over him and articulated the words very carefully, as if she was addressing a slightly dense child. "It means every time you are awake and you don't have to go to work, you come here. Do you understand?" She straightened up and typed something else. "Besides, the system calculated that in this way it will take a lot less time to extinguish your debt."

"How long?" inquired Hank.

"However long you have left to live should be sufficient," she replied with a reptilian smile.

Hank was anchored to the desk with his hands.

"Ah. Well...if it's the only way..."

"I can't find any other resolution, Mr. B. Provided that obviously there is a true desire, on your part, to pay off the debt," reiterated the lady, almost casually. "Otherwise, you'll have to deal with the penalty provided by the judicial system in such circumstances."

"Of course, there's the desire," repeated Hank, swallowing noisily.

The lady typed away on the keyboard and produced a new window from the monitor; it was structured in the form of a contract that she slid under his nose with a casual movement of her index finger. At the bottom of the page, a horizontal line rested blank next to the date that was flashing in red.

"With a signature here, you declare you're transferring your free time to the State as compensation for non-payment to the State, itself," she announced, passing him an electronic pen. "I can't guarantee this is going to be immediate, but it will certainly take less time than cutting your salary. From which, by the way, you'll have to remember to deduct the current Existence Taxation, otherwise you'll always find yourself short and all of this work will be rendered futile," she softly reminded him.

"Of course," stammered Hank.

He took the pen in his hand, stunned by the ease with which a matter like that had been resolved, and signed his name in the air, on the flashing line, in an unsteady calligraphy.

"Perfect," said the lady. "Now, another one here, and here..." she instructed, making another two, almost identical, papers appear. "Then we just need your fingerprints..."

A third window emerged, blossoming with two massive scanners on which Hank pressed both his thumbs. He must have been sporting quite a miserable face, because the impeccable lady seemed to feel obliged to comfort him.

"Cheer up, Mr. B, you're not the first who has opted for this solution and you won't be the last," she said, while the screen uploaded his files. "Bumps in the road can always occur, but with good will, one can always find a way."

"Can I go back to my apartment?" asked Hank, feeling light-headed.

"Absolutely," the lady replied, showing her gums. "It's yours by right."

The computer responded with a beeping sound, and Hank's fingerprints lit up in green.

"You're all set."

"That's it?"

"Your dossier has been uploaded in the system and it's already been placed in another category," confirmed the lady. The screen went white.

Hank had no idea it could be so easy. He didn't even have the time to think. He scratched his head, still feeling confused.

"What do I do now?"

"Do you usually start your shift at the factory, by this time?"

"No, I'd be free right now. Today I begin work after lunch."

"Great. In that case, you can start immediately. Sit down."

Hank looked around, puzzled. The room was crammed full of a new batch of people, and some who were there before were still waiting. The toddler had resumed his whining. A short distance from the desk, on the left, there was a free, ugly, plastic chair, not dissimilar to the others that filled the room.

"Do I have to sit down?"

"Sit down, Mr. Bradshaw."

The chair was nothing out of the ordinary. It was full of scratches from over-use, dull-coloured, holding the promise of back pain. Hank pointed at it with his finger.

"Do I have to sit there?"

"There, Mr. Bradshaw," the lady slowly repeated.

She followed him with her eyes, until Hank was seated on the ugly plastic chair with his hands on his knees. Then, she smiled at him baring her gums, diverted her gaze and pushed the button for the next customer.

Hank looked to his right, then to his left.

Sighing, he stretched his legs out in front of him.

# HOT HEADS

Robbie was put down gently. The wooden framing at the base of the window put out an unexpected warmth, compared to the cold silver of the tray on which he had been delivered. Maybe they had installed one of those radiation panel systems, or something like that. He was feeling numb, and he asked himself how it could be possible. It must have had something to do with that ghost limb thing the doctors had told him about. In front of him, beyond the glass, the asphalt of a common highway was boiling, and, on the other side of the sidewalk, he could see the peeling wall of a building bathed in a light made sickly pink by fine dust. Three pairs of eyes rotated in his direction. An eloquent silence followed.

"What happened to you?" the Old Man finally asked.

He had a mane of salt and pepper hair, cut unevenly, and his face looked to have been carved by a plough. The Girl with the long brown hair flashed an encouraging smile at him. Her eyes were shining with an emerald glow.

"Motorbike accident," Robbie explained with a sigh. "Head-on collision with a truck. The driver dozed off. I don't remember anything. I woke up in the hospital two weeks after the procedure."

"Who signed the consent form for the procedure?" asked The Noblewoman.

Her head was topped by an elaborate hairdo that seemed to hold itself up, rigid as scaffolding.

"My girlfriend."

"Are you okay with that?" inquired The Old Man.

Robbie turned his head to the side.

"It's okay, I think," he mumbled. "Better than being stone-dead in a morgue freezer, I guess. Well, actually, I still have to get used to it. I got out of the hospital just this weekend, and once home..."

"...You found the letter of employment from the Ministry waiting for you. With all the best wishes, immediate and with no appeal," concluded The Old Man.

"What a rip-off."

"Why are you always so argumentative?" warbled The Noblewoman.

She was wearing earrings that, by the looks of them, must have cost more than Robbie's motorbike. The right one was hanging crooked, on the verge of coming out of her earlobe; the other, hung straight.

"In my case, I requested it myself," she revealed. "I was perfectly conscious when my doctor informed me of this possibility. The metastasis already spread to many areas of my body, but my brain activity was perfectly normal. This way, it will take a few more years before my relatives can fight over my inheritance!"

A grunt sprung from The Old Man's lips. The Noblewoman ignored it.

"Besides..." she said haughtily, "I find it to be an honourable decision. Everyone has to make his contribution to the growth of the community to the best of their abilities. Take that special needs group. Their association puts them to work cleaning the streets. It's a nice thing, isn't it? I believe that what we are doing is an act of fairness and civic duty at the same time. We may be disabled, but we're still useful members of society!"

The Old Man clicked his tongue in mockery.

"I just thought I had more choices," said Robbie. "I mean, more options."

"My dear boy, I don't know if you had a job before the accident," replied The Noblewoman in a measured and rational tone, "but I assume you found it based on your qualifications. You couldn't always have it your way! Now, in your condition, the choice has been narrowed down a bit, but you have to admit They are trying to do what they can."

"It's just that I never thought I would have ended up doing this job," admitted Robbie.

"Better than being idle," replied The Noblewoman, pompously.

A man wearing a hat and a turquoise scarf who was walking in a hurry, heading who-knows where, slowed down in front of the window and lingered to watch them briefly, before stepping away with an indecipherable expression.

Robbie turned to The Girl, who had been silent thus far.

"And how did you end up here?"

She lowered her heavy eyelids.

"I stopped eating," she said, with a voice so soft Robbie almost had to ask her to say it again.

"Okay," he agreed, "and how did the transition from your diet to your present condition take place?"

"Rupture of the esophagus," she whispered.

"I understand," he replied, not actually understanding in the slightest. "Did your family persuade you?"

The Girl nodded, sucking in her already hollowed cheekbones. An intermittent red glint cut through the shadow between her jawbone and neck, as if her skin became rhythmically inflamed with a reddish, unnatural rash.

"My mum said she wasn't ready to let me go. They assured her I could lead a normal life."

The Old Man let out a neigh like huff.

"Were you aware this was going to be your destiny?"

"No, but I am happy that my parents signed me up for the procedure," she murmured. "It's the best thing for me, I mean. Not having a body."

"And do you think the result was worth it?" the Old Man intervened sardonically. "Is this your idea of a 'normal life'?"

The Girl lowered her eyes, hurt.

"What do you see that's abnormal in this?" The Noblewoman attacked him.

"All of it!"

"What you define as abnormal is called *progress!*"

The Old Man turned to Robbie.

"I didn't ask for this," he said. "I didn't have a crumb of decision making in this whole affair. It was my children who decided for me, while I was unconscious in a hospital bed."

"Coma?"

"Myocardial infarction," replied The Old Man. "According to my kids, I am here by the skin of my teeth. When I woke up like this, they were at my bedside, all happy. As far as I am concerned, they should have minded their own damn business."

"You don't like being here?" ventured Robbie.

"Quiet, everyone!" rebuked The Noblewoman in a hiss.

From behind them echoed a click-clack of approaching footsteps, then a hand reached out to smooth The Old Man's uneven tuft of hair. A thumb and an index finger with trimmed nails went towards The Noblewoman and gently straightened her right earring. The Noblewoman followed the movements of those fingers quietly, with a worshipping gaze of silence and lingering gratitude. The footsteps moved away.

"It's the supervisor," elucidated The Noblewoman. "She can't stand talking during the work shift. It frightens the customers, and such."

The Old Man turned to Robbie, his forehead like a treasure map.

"Do you understand what I mean, now, kiddo? Stuck here for ten hours, and we're not even allowed to utter a peep!"

"Oh, please!" scoffed the Noblewoman. "At the factory, would you just start chatting at your leisure during your working hours?"

The Old Man shot her a surly glance.

"Maybe to you this stunt seems charitable like one of your fundraising dinners, my dear, but I have been a slave my whole life, and, given my condition, I don't think it's too much to ask to be left in peace."

The Noblewoman snapped like a snake.

"Oh, stop it! What would you prefer? To sit all day long on your grandson's chest of drawers like a useless ornament, is that what you'd rather do?"

"I'd rather DIE," snarled The Old Man, his voice penetrating with such violence that The Girl flinched.

She got so upset, she started to cry. Thick tears rolled down her cheeks and gathered in the slope of her neckline. And suddenly, she began to sizzle.

It started like a spasmodic tic, a subtle movement of the head. The Girl blinked an eyelid, and for the briefest moment, Robbie thought she was winking at him, an assumption that filled him with a guilty sensation of enticement. Then, her eyes widened until they bulged out, frog-like, and she started bouncing with the rhythmic buzzing of a dental drill: a frenzied, twitchy dance that made her collapse to one side of her face, while small electric sparks crackled on her eyelids and the tip of her ears. Black smoke started rising from below.

"Oh dear!" uttered The Noblewoman fearfully, her squeal muffled by the piercing cry of a siren.

The Girl continued vibrating in silence, shrouded in smoke, her thick, swollen tongue hanging out, touching the floor, her eyes popping out of their sockets, darting back and forth in different directions. Her hair stuck out straight from her head. From behind her came barely contained curses, then an alarmed click-clack of footsteps hurried in. Two strong hands lowered on either side of The Girl, searching around her electrified hair, down her neck. The siren abruptly stopped, leaving a silence as deafening as the unbearable blaring.

The Girl stopped trembling immediately, stiffening at first, then deflating. She didn't move anymore at all. The tears evaporated from her cheeks, her eyes askew, fixed on different directions.

The two hands lifted The Girl by the ears out of visual range and took her away. The air was brimming with a nauseating fragrance of static and burned hair. In the empty space left by The Girl, lingered a light, dust-free impression in the form of a circle.

There was a brief moment of pitiful silence.

"Nice extortion job, huh?" growled The Old Man finally. "Progress. For one reason or another, you're given up for dead, but *progress* found a way to let you survive. When the body is not responding anymore, but by sheer luck your brain has not been reduced to pulp, here comes progress to the rescue, allowing you to postpone the final goodbye! Well, many congratulations. But don't forget, kid, that progress is not a gift, it's a debt. And just like any debt, it has to be paid. If we keep you alive, you have to do something for us that goes beyond pure living. Fuck just living. The solution is at your disposal, but you have to earn it. You have to be functional. Disabled, yes, but a functional disabled. Get to work. You *must* work, otherwise you're not just handicapped, you are a handicapped parasite, and what good is spending money and energy to save the skin of a handicapped parasite? Imagine...imagine when they finally invent the recipe for eternal life, when it's already been consumed by the rich and they've discovered how to profit from selling it on an industrial scale - then you will get to spend your eternal life earning a living!"

The Old Man was shouting now, fueled by his own thoughts.

The click-clack of footsteps returned, menacingly this time, and, once perceiving a restored silence, retreated.

"Existence is a badly stipulated contract made by those who came before you," sentenced The Old Man, wheezing like a nag.

"But..." feebly bleated The Noblewoman. Her right earring had come off the earlobe again, and was laying sadly, next to the electronic device fixed around the base of her neck. "... the contribution to the community... making a difference..."

"I PISS on making a difference!" roared The Old Man foaming at the mouth.

He spat with scorn.

The spittle dribbled down the window of the wig shop with the desperate sluggishness of snail mucus.

# PERSISTENCE

per·sis·tence (per-sĭs′tens)

*n.*

1. The act of persisting.
2. The state or quality of being persistent; persistency.
3. <u>Continuance of an effect after the cause is removed.</u>

The body lies flat on the rug in the middle of the living room floor, face turned in the opposite direction. This way, at least, they don't have to look him in the eyes.

Andy is still breathing heavily. The ashtray he used to strike the blow has fallen from his hands and rolled across the floor, to Ava's feet. Her hands are covering her mouth, but she did not scream, and her presence of mind prevented the neighbours from coming and knocking on their door, asking if everything was ok.

Time seems to stand still while they both calm down, panting, recovering from the shock.

After all, it doesn't happen every day that you kill your landlord.

"I think I'll do a line," Ava eventually said, with a broken voice.

The room around Andy started spinning, and he found himself on the floor, folded in two. He hears a chopping rhythm hovering somewhere above him, but he can't really listen. He realises he might be experiencing some sort of panic attack. Finally, he hears a sniffing sound, and that rattles him a little. Trembling, Andy reaches for his powdery, white goal line on his hands and knees. They snort two feet away from the supine body.

After a couple lines, Andy bounces back and starts to see more clearly again.

Ava's voice echoes in the silent room.

"What do we do?"

Now, that. The old man's body hasn't moved yet, but where would he go, after all? He's dead as a doornail. They made him so, *he* made him so. Andy suddenly remembers the ashtray, and he picks it up. It feels heavy in his hands and has traces of clotted blood around the rim. It must be covered in fingerprints. He clumsily reaches for a napkin and starts to wipe the ashtray with it.

"We need to stay focused," he says. "We'll get through it, we just have to fix this, one step at a time."

"They're gonna find out that his car has been here, today. Someone in the neighbourhood must have spotted it."

"Ok, ok. Here's how it went: the guy came by, asked for rent money from us, we kindly begged him to postpone payment, he accepts, he drives away in his car, period. End of the story. We don't know what happened next."

"Wait. Doesn't the dude have a cellphone, or something?" Ava asks lamely. "Aren't those things, like, traceable? Hell, they may be recording this very conversation, right now."

"I'll handle it," Andy replies. "First, we have to dispose of the body."

"I watched a documentary on this serial killer," Ava murmurs, expressionless. "He cut his victims' bodies into pieces and put them in the freezer."

"What?!" Andy utters. "Are you out of your mind?"

"Can't you do anything, besides criticising?" Ava spits venomously. Her face is as pale as the surface of the moon.

"Just saying', let's explore all our options here," Andy says, trying to sound professional, though clearly on the verge of losing it. "I'm not butchering the dude, that's an honour I'll leave to you, if you're so eager for it." Ava suddenly appears uncertain. "Besides, what about the blood? It's gonna get everywhere."

"We could do it in the bathtub," Ava suggests, in the same toneless voice.

They ended up wrapping him in the rug, after stripping him of his wallet and car keys, and stashed him in the closet like some kind of heavy burrito. They sweat buckets trying to lay him down, only to discover that he doesn't fit, so they struggle to stand him upright. It's almost as if the body knows they're the enemies and is engaged in a battle, it doesn't stay upright and keeps threatening to fall on their heads. It takes a lot of work, but in the end, they manage to balance him in a corner, between a shelf and a large cardboard box full of junk. Ava pulls out a battered tarp from somewhere and covers him with it.

Back in the kitchen, they find a stain. The rug was slick with blood. Not much, just a spot where the blood flowed out of the wound in his head, but dense enough to seep through the material and stain the wooden floor beneath. They helplessly look at it, then at each other.

"I'll get the mop," Ava says eventually.

They scrubbed the spot vigorously for a long time, but the stain still seemed to them to have left a sort of dark halo on the wooden floor.

"It's just wet," Andy pants as they rest, balanced on their heels. "It will dry."

Ava savagely bites her nails.

"His car is still outside."

Andy stands, feeling dizzy. He picks up the landlord's wallet from the table, snaps in half all the credit cards he finds but keeps the cash. Then, he grabs the man's car keys.

"Burn it all," he says, before leaving. "I'll take care of the car."

*

Ava curls up next to Andy in bed that night. Since he returned, empty-handed and without giving any explanations, she has been brisk, silent and business-like in her behavior, so Andy takes her in his arms, thinking they will both benefit from the release of stress. Despite all of his efforts, though, she is awfully quiet during their lovemaking, and he has to admit he too was distracted. It's not even that he isn't in the mood, it's that there's a big elephant in the room, lying in bed right in the middle of them, so this is basically a threesome.

"Sorry," he mumbles, before rolling away.

She tucks her head beneath his armpit, and they lie there like that, without speaking.

"I wish we could just, like, disappear," Ava whispers, after a while.

Andy rolls on his side to face her. Her mouth is a severe, tight line.

"Babe," he murmurs, "nobody wanted it to go this far. Things got out of hand, sure. But we needed the money. For the dope. We still owe people, 'member? We couldn't keep paying his old greedy ass, and for what? This rathole he calls a house?"

"Dude's only luck in life was owning this house," she sighs.

"Besides, we can't change the past," Andy underlines. "Now we have to think past this. To what is best for us, to keep going. Alright?"

Ava bites her lip and says nothing.

*

He is at work when he gets the call. His counsellor had found him this job, after months of begging and the results of a fake clean drug test. He was delivering newspapers, newspapers that no one reads anymore because of the progress of technology, but he receives a small percentage of what he sells. It isn't great, but at least he has managed not to screw it up, and he prides himself on that small victory.

"The police came by," Ava says on the phone, and he can tell by the sound of her voice that she's been biting her nails.

"How many of them?"

"Just two."

"Did they, you know." Andy hears his voice lowering of his own initiative, and he let his eyes roam around. It's a normal busy afternoon street, still he starts to feel a little squeamish. "Did they ask any questions?"

"The usual, I guess - him being our landlord and all."

"Did they snoop around?"

"Nah, we stayed in the living room. I made coffee and we had a chat. They wanted to know who lived in the house and for how long, and such. They want to speak with you, too. I tried to stick to the DL, but..." she emitted a funny noise, like a choked sob. "I nearly lost it. I don't know what to do, Andy. I need you here, now."

"Baby, it's ok. Try to stay calm. I'm on my way."

"Something came in the mail, today." Her voice is jittery, high-pitched with anguish.

"What is it?"

"It's the rent."

"The rent?!"

That's impossible.

Dude's dead, he can't send his threatening letters anymore.

He never came to collect the rent in person. Every damn month he mailed the same damn white envelope. On the back, he always wrote the name of the sender, to avoid all doubt; on the inside, he put a bank deposit form, that they were supposed to fill out and go pay. It's just that, after a while, they had stopped paying. One month they were too lazy, the other, too stoned. The one after, too broke. That was fine for a while, and they even thought they'd get away just smooth with it, until the old man went to his bank and realised he was short a lot of money. Those envelopes were actually the main reason he showed up in person: they had been ignoring him for too long.

"It's probably a mistake," Andy grumbled. "Maybe it's the one from last month, or he put it in the mailbox before coming in the house, you know he's nuts."

There followed a brief silence. Ava must have been chewing her nails to the roots.

"I'm coming. Forget about it. Throw it away."

Andy blew off work halfway through. On his way home, he threw the remaining unsold newspapers into a trash can.

*

The rug in the closet had started to smell. Andy could whiff it through the closed door. Plus, every time he looked at that faint stain on the wooden floor, his head would spin.

"We need to get rid of that," he told Ava one day, meaning the body. She had already popped a couple of pills and was idly scrolling through her phone, her favourite pastime since they had sold the tv.

"Yeah, how do you reckon?" she slurred.

On his way out, Andy noticed that the mailbox was full. The mailman had dropped off three common white envelopes. Frowning, Andy grabbed one. On the back, he saw the name of the sender written in black ink.

"You got to be kidding..." He ripped it open, and he discovered the same blank deposit form that had been haunting them for months.

What if the old man had given someone the job to send the rent trying wear them down until they paid? A company, maybe? This was getting ridiculous.

He balled up the envelopes and kicked them into the sewer drain outside.

*

Andy went to the police station in person. Ava couldn't remember the names of the officers who came visiting, or maybe she had never known in the first place, so he just told someone at the front desk why he was there. After an endless wait, he was directed into a squalid office, where he waited again, until two men showed up.

"Are you gonna record this?" he can't help but ask.

"I don't know. Are you going to tell us something interesting?" the younger policeman retorts.

Andy tried to laugh, but really, it was a grimace. They asked him more or less the same questions they had asked Ava: his relationship to the landlord, the last time he had seen him, if he ever noticed any "strange" behaviour. They were straight forward, but in a good enough mood.

"So, any news yet?" he daringly asks when it seems they had finished.

"Not at the moment, no. He might be wandering around in a confused state. He's elderly, and he lives alone. We're trying to get in touch with his son, but there are seven different time zones between us and him."

"Well, thing is... not sure what to do about the house," Andy adds. "Like, 'til he turns up... can we stay? I mean, it's not like we know where to go... like, we remain, waiting for somebody to tell us something..."

"Just make sure you stay available, for any eventuality."

"Yeah, but we just stay in the house, or, like, how do we manage?"

The officers shared a glance.

"We don't know what to say."

Nobody knows what to say. Andy left the police station feeling cheated. They may have bought his story and he had worn his good clothes, but cops are cops, and he's sure they can recognise a junkie when they see one. He knew that he reeked of junkie, or maybe it's just the reek of suspicion.

He found Ava on the couch. She was high as a kite and staring at their houseplant. She insisted they buy it to make the house look nicer, but they gradually had stopped taking care of it, and now it was wilting.

"Look at that leaf," she said, sounding detached. "How hard it tries to attach itself to that branch. Can you imagine the amount of effort it takes just to do that? Just to hang on?"

"Ava, let's go to bed."

There were six envelopes on the table, next to the plant. They had found them that very morning in the mailbox, and they were using them as coasters, staining them with food and coffee. Andy took the envelopes and tore them up, one after the other.

\*

He developed a phobia about looking in the mailbox. It would be so much easier just to ignore it and pretend it wasn't an issue. Every time he looked at it, his legs felt heavy with fear and remorse.

Envelopes kept on arriving on a regular basis, all plain white ones with the landlord's name written on the back and a blank form inside. He got rid of them every time, hiding them from Ava who was getting edgier day by day, but he was not always lucky.

Once, he went out to take care of a job and he shot his usual frightened glance at the mailbox. His courage was rewarded with a sense of relief, because it was empty. When he came back, though, he opened the door on an already freaked out Ava.

There was a pile of envelopes spread across the couch. She had found them in the mailbox while going out for cigarettes, and she was rambling about how "they" knew about the whole story, and of a hypothetical blackmailing police operation through this envelope system to force them to confess.

Uselessly, Andy tried to steer the conversation back onto a logical track.

"You've been snorting too much coke, and it's made you paranoid."

"Stop belittling me. We have a *corpse* rotting in our closet, Andy!"

"Will you keep your voice down?" Andy half snarled, half begged; but she was too far gone to care.

"That body needs to go."

"We agreed we're going to do something about it. If we bring him..."

"I am NOT touching that thing," she cried out hysterically.

Andy lost his cool. "So, the problem is not the body, the problem is *you* not wanting to cooperate!"

She screamed even louder.

"I *TOLD* you I don't want to..."

Andy banged his fist on the table so violently the ashtray jumped.

"That's all you can do, huh? Tell me what you *don't* want and act like you're *not* involved, but you know what? *You were there.* Doing things. You agreed with this, so you're in it as much as I am. You are as guilty as I am."

His outburst silenced her. She stood there, her face a mask of tears and snot.

"Maybe we should turn ourselves in," she murmured. "Those envelopes keep on coming, and that body. I can't close my eyes without seeing it. I see it in my dreams, I see it when I'm awake. I just can't stand being in the same house with it. It's either him or me."

Andy pitied that pathetic face. He grabbed her wet cheeks in his hands.

"I'll handle it. Ok? If I promise you, I've got this, will you calm down?"

Ava weakly nodded, but she couldn't stop shaking.

"It's gone," she says.

"What?"

She pointed to the houseplant. The leaf fell to the ground, and the branch is now bare. Ava stared at it, grieving.

"I should have watered it more."

He shook her.

"Come on, I'll make you some coffee."

Before going to bed, Andy grabbed the pile of crumpled letters from the couch and flushed them down the toilet.

*

He called Pete, of course he called Pete. He was the guy who took care of the car, and if he asked for a lot of money to do that, god knows what this other task was going to cost. Andy still didn't know how he was going to pay for this. He felt the noose of debt tightening around his neck. Pete arrived in the early afternoon with his big cousin, both dressed up like workers. Andy led them to the closet. Ava sat on the living room couch, dried houseplant by her side, and glancing worriedly at them while sucking on a cigarette.

The rug was soaked with a viscous, greasy substance that smelled like death. Pete and his cousin wore gloves, they produced two large black plastic garbage bags. While Andy held one open, they slowly lowered the body into it, then covering the exposed body parts with the other one. Andy felt like puking, but the cousins do not even flinch. He kept his head turned away as he held the bag open.

They secured the sack with a tie and they carried it out on their shoulders. Andy opened the door to the shared hallway for them. Down all seven steps of the stairs they descended from their landing to the front door, Andy anxiously waited for someone to come down from the upper floors. Through closed curtains, he observed the cousins load the sack onto a small garbage truck Pete had managed to snag from the junkyard, and then they jumped into the vehicle. Only then, did he dare to go out onto the sidewalk to say goodbye with a nod of his head.

"Yo, someone in your building needs to pick up their mail," Pete said.

Andy felt a chill crawl down his spine. He went to check the mailbox. It was overflowing with letters. The whole mailbox looked swollen on the verge of exploding. As soon as he opened the small door, an avalanche of envelopes fell at his feet. They all bore the same name and address of the sender, and they all contained blank bank deposit forms. Andy tried to pick them all up, but there were so many, they kept slipping from his hands and he realised that he had to make multiple trips. He came and went until he got them all, then he ran his hands on the inside of the mailbox just to make sure, and once in the house he threw the whole pile into the kitchen sink and set them on fire with a lighter. Ava stayed curled up on the sofa, smoking weed. She flicked her ashes into the dried houseplant.

*

That night, he dreamed of bodies. He was at a party full of people, booze and dope. Loud music was blasting from gigantic speakers, and he weaved his way past various faceless bodies passed out on the floor. Everybody seemed to be having a good time and the atmosphere was exciting and giddy, though slightly disconcerting, as if there was something not right. Then he spotted him, fair hair tucked under his usual beanie cap. He was chatting with a strange man wearing a hat and a turquoise scarf. Andy approached him.

"Marty?"

He turned around. He had soft eyes and a yellow smile, and had a pen stuck in his left arm.

"I'm kicking it!" Marty said, before he started retching onto the rug.

His vomit was dense and white, dotted with black globs that landed on the thick fabric. Rivulets of black dribble on the dusty rug pattern.

Suddenly, Andy realised they are partying in his closet, and the space felt narrow, hot and claustrophobic.

He turned around and Marty's body was now sprawled on the floor, in the same position that the cleaning people had found him that morning, in the toilet at the train station. But now, his front was ripped open, bleeding from the edges of his cuts, and his guts were exposed, and they were made of throbbing envelopes, as if he was a sack of meat belonging to the postal service. All the other bodies lying around were split in half and oozing ropy, milky matter.

Andy felt something stuck in his throat and gagged. Acid climbed up his esophagus, he hunched over and vomited a wrinkled ball of paper swarming with typed words, alive, swirling and writhing like fat, infesting worms.

He was awakened by a soft, insistent tapping at the door. He got up and open it, wild-eyed. The mailman, a tall, lanky red-haired guy, looked at him half-frightened, half-amazed.

"It's just that... your mailbox is overflowing," he exclaimed, pointing down the hallway with his thumb. "I was about to leave your mail on your doormat, but then I knocked, just to make sure somebody was still living here. I thought you might have moved, or something."

Andy rushed to the mailbox. There were so many envelopes that the pressure had broken the worn-out latch, and the door was open, spewing out a messy stack of white paper envelopes onto the floor. More of them were bundled up inside the box, torn, folded, crumpled, some still pristine and intact.

A horrible wave of anguish hit Andy to his core, tightening his throat and the pit of his stomach, and he perceived his body switching immediately to a fight or flight mode. He felt like all the joy of being alive had been sucked out of him by a ravenous straw.

"No... no, no, no!" he viciously tore the envelopes, ripping them to confetti, but the more he tore, the more they seem to multiply.

Envelopes kept on coming out, as if the mailbox was an endless dark pit that had swallowed gigantic amounts of material, that were now floating back to the surface.

In an instant, he found himself surrounded by white shredded paper as still more crumpled letters were peeking from the box. Andy was almost reduced to tears, feeling impotent. He rushed back into the house, panicked, leaving the mess behind. Ava sat on the sofa, staring at the houseplant.

"We need to go."

She blinked at him, face blank.

"What?"

He was already out of sight. Ava followed him into the bedroom. He had picked up a battered backpack, and was stuffing pants, t-shirts and other random belongings into it.

"What are you doing?"

"We need to scram. Get your things and let's go!"

"But the police said we have to stay put..."

"Forget it. We're leaving. I'm gonna call Pete and ask for a fake ID. We're gonna disappear and start all over again. That's what you wanted, after all, right?"

"Andy, slow down, will ya? You're scaring me."

Andy became irritated. He felt as if he had no time for this.

"Why does everything have to be so fucking difficult, with you? Why aren't you capable of thinking quickly, to decide? I'm sick of trying to clean up your mess! Do as I say, for once, and pack your things."

"No."

"What?" Andy hissed, turning to face her.

She was trembling, standing in the middle of the room. Her face was a wax mask.

"You really want me to make a decision, well, that's it. I'm going to confess."

Andy felt like fainting.

"Ava, no."

"Yes. I'm gonna tell them everything. Everything we did."

"You can't do that! You can't screw me over!"

"What else am I supposed to do?" she started to cry.

Andy moved a step towards her, and she backed off.

"Come with me. We're gonna leave town, get clean. Keep a low profile, for a while. We'll forget all about this. We'll start from scratch!"

"I can't!" Ava frantically screamed, and now tears were streaming down her face. "Stop manipulating me! I fucking can't forget, and I can't keep on doing this. I can't keep hanging on, I need to let it go!"

She put on a stern face and looked at him, dead serious. "I'm going. And nothing you can say is gonna make me change my mind."

It all happened in the blink of an eye.

Ava turned to leave. Andy launched himself forward and grabbed her by the arm. She fought back, trying to scratch him with her free hand, aiming for his eyes. Andy shoved her forcefully, letting her out of his grip. Ava stumbled backwards, tripping on her own feet, and fell. Her head hit the corner of a cabinet. She collapsed to the floor like a ragdoll and lay still.

Andy felt a punch to his guts, and for a moment he saw black. He was hyper-ventilating. His body moved on his own accord, and he found himself crouched next to her. Her eyes were wide open, and she wasn't breathing. Andy heard the loud sobbing before he realised that it was coming from him. His throat closed, his lungs gasped for air and he was shaking badly. He felt hot tears start flowing, now, through the thick, grey fog that was clouding his head. He was totally destroyed; his whole body shook from sobbing. He felt as if he had reached the point of no return. *Here I go*, he thought, *now I'm going crazy.*

He didn't go crazy. When the outlines become sharper, he got back on his feet, filled with dread. He was afraid to touch anything, thoughts spun through his mind like a rollercoaster: it's mostly about fingerprints, along with the envelopes, and the stain on the floor, and that fucking houseplant...he needed to think straight. He picked up his backpack, then rummaged through Ava's purse and took all the cash he could find. He left everything else, grabbed his jacket and the car keys and closed the door behind him. The hall was deserted and quiet. There was still a carpet of torn envelopes on the floor. Andy left it all behind, without looking back.

Outside, it was getting dark. It was a beautiful fall evening, one of those where the light lingers just a little bit longer, clinging strenuously to the summer just gone, and the headlights of distant cars sparkled in a velvety blue canvas that gradually darkened.

It's all so beautiful and profoundly unfair.

Leaning on the bridge railing, Andy felt ill and observed life. He chain-smoked cigarettes and craved with grief and longing his old dull routine, the blissful nothingness of empty days. He felt like crying, but he had no tears left. He didn't even get the luxury of madness; he had to face his shit and get it together. He memorised Pete's number before tossing his phone in the river.

He drove his rundown car to a seedy motel on the outskirts of town where he wouldn't be asked for identification and checked in under a false name. He was given an anonymous room with a view of the road, and it smelled like stale and low-cost detergent. Andy filled his lungs with that stench, finding it strangely comforting. He smoked on the balcony. The lights of a diner winked at him from the other side of the road. He knew he should eat something, but he felt queasy, like someone had tied his stomach in a knot. He went out and called Pete from a pay phone. Pete picked up on the fifth ring. They fixed an appointment at the junkyard for the next day, no questions asked. He hung up and rested his head on the receiver.

Suddenly, a strange urge to laugh bubbled up in his throat. It was the last ray of sunshine, a faint glimpse of hope shining through despair. Maybe not everything was lost. Pete's a good guy. He'll offer to work for him and repay everything he owes. He'll find a way. When you're alive, you can always find a way. For the first time that day, he felt the noose loosen up a little bit.

He thought about that diner on the other side of the street, but a residual pang of fear kicked back at him, and he was still afraid he'd throw up anything he swallowed, nicotine aside. He didn't want to be alone, but he couldn't be around people either. Maybe he'd go back to his room, lie down a little bit and turn on the TV, for company. Then, if he felt like it, he'd grab a bite at that diner. He tried not to think too far ahead. Baby steps, just to survive.

He slowly went back to the motel. The road lay in complete darkness now, dimly lit by the dirty light of some occasional lamppost. In the hallway, he tried to smile at the receptionist, who didn't even spare him a second glance.

He swiped the card in the door lock. The room was half in the dark and cold. He had left the curtains opened, and an anaemic stream of light shone on something lying face down on the bedsheet.

Andy moved closer.

An envelope, pale as the face of a bloodless man, was silently waiting for him, like a lover slouched on a cheap duvet. The handwritten name of the sender stood out against all the whiteness, bleeding black ink onto a blank paper skin.

# THE POISON

On a day like any other, Max Strumann was urgently rushed to the hospital with severe stomach pain.

He had been suffering from a fierce burning sensation for weeks, but he had supposed it was a symptom of his gastritis. After the residents' meeting, though, the pain had sent him back home literally folded in two. He had dragged himself, step after step, up the stairs to his apartment, up to his bathroom, where he arrived more dead than alive; it was then that his wife had called an ambulance.

From the medical report, he found out with astonishment that he was the victim of thallium poisoning. The doctors were more surprised than he was. A group of them showed up at his bedside, asking information about what he had eaten recently, and if he usually drank tap or bottled water. Max listed his eating habits, pointing out he didn't recall doing anything out of the ordinary.

"Well, it is odd."

They were all puzzled. Questioned on the subject, Max's wife confirmed she had been eating the same meals as Max every day, and nothing had happened to her, not even a stomach ache.

Eventually, the blame fell on the beer served in Gunnel's bar, where Max went every Friday after work, and where that very evening a proper inspection took place. The place was cleared out, wrapped like a Christmas gift, and the door sealed. The customers' chatter flooded the sidewalk, and reached Max's ears in the person of his brother-in-law, a regular there, who came to visit him in the hospital, informing him that Gunnel was ruined. Gunnel herself felt compelled to pay him a visit, almost in tears; she swore up and down that in over thirty years in the business, never, ever had anything like this happened, neither voluntarily, nor by mistake; also, she didn't remember putting out rat poison, the only substance that could contain thallium, from its place on the lowest shelf behind the bar, where she kept it, separated from the other bottles meant for the customers. Max firmly believed that she was innocent, especially as his brother-in-law, that infamous night, had taken a sip from his own mug and he was fit as a fiddle. By then, unfortunately, the damage was done, anyway. Max was admitted to a single room and seemed to recover quickly.

"How are you feeling today, Mr. Strumann?"

The doctor appeared at the door, smiling friendly. Max raised his gaze from his book.

"I feel better."

"All your vitals have stabilised, after pumping your stomach. I'd say you're safe."

"Yeah, I do, I-I think I feel fine."

"I am happy to announce that tomorrow, you will be discharged."

That afternoon, Max decided to take a little trip to the cafeteria. The hallway echoed with solitary coughing, it was depressing, and almost deserted. From a half-opened door, Max caught a glimpse of an exasperated nurse, who was changing an IV with brisk, hurried gestures. A little further on, a bald man had just bent over to take a beverage from the vending machine. Straightening up, he bumped into a messy little woman. She was bundled up in a scarf, and walking hurriedly, stumbling on her heels. Brown, muddy liquid spilt from the paper cup the man was holding, and plummeted to the floor, splashing on his clothes. The woman seemed not to even notice and kept on walking without a word of apology. The bald man was left to stare after her, his fingers dripping, throwing curses behind her back.

Max felt a faint cramp in his stomach.

The cafeteria was crowded. Its walls were white, but filthy. While Max was standing in a corner, two men in white coats promptly arrived from the hallway, going directly to the counter, jumping to the front of the long line. The food worker served them immediately.

"Excuse me, it was my turn!" a woman at the front of the line reprimanded.

The server casted her a bored glance.

"Yeah? I'll be with you in a minute."

She scoffed, in disbelief.

"But it's my turn. Now. I was here first."

"I told you I'll be with you in a minute," the food worker replied, polemically. "Can you do me a favor and wait a minute? Can you do that?"

"Is this a joke?" the woman looked astounded. "This is fucking unbelievable!"

She grabbed her purse, livid, and left the cafeteria without placing her order.

The two white coats' gaze followed her, their faces sporting the look of someone who's observing a vile and miserable creature.

"Someone's a little upset today," the younger white coat said.

"I'm no expert, but it's probably a case of female problems," sniggered the server.

"I hope for her sake that she never finds herself in line to be visited by me," the oldest white coat commented, sipping his drink. He was the kind of man who took for himself an abnormal space on the train seats, because the thought of having to share a slice of reality with other people offended his reason. "I assure you; her turn would never come."

The younger white coat burst out laughing.

Max collapsed to the cafeteria floor, foaming at the mouth.

After his relapse, he spent another few weeks in the ward for further tests. They conducted an inspection in the hospital cafeteria, but it was a dead end. Max couldn't do anything else but wait, until they considered him well again. The day of his hospital discharge, his wife gave him a ride home before she went to work, and he spent the whole morning in the house, reading books on poetry. At some point in the afternoon, he wanted to go out and get some fresh air.

At the front door, he ran into the old woman who lived on the first floor, whose only aspect of her life he came to know, was the sight of the edge of her wooden imperial-style cabinet, the only piece of furniture her heavy door chain allowed anyone to see each time she cracked open her front door. She was accompanied by her grim and unavoidable Pekinese dog with crooked teeth. The old bat had been told by Max's wife, of his hospitalisation. She offered him her congratulations on his recovery, and she investigated the plausible causes of his sickness, declaring she was not amazed at all by the ambiguity of the situation.

"Nowadays nothing makes sense anymore," she commented, choking her dog while pulling his leash in the attempt to remove him from a hedge. "With all of these people who come to live here from who knows where, with all their habits, we have no antibodies. You never know what germs you'll pick up."

Wrinkling her lips already dried with lipstick, the old bat bulged her eyes out in the eloquent way of someone looking for an ally in a worrisome situation. Actually, she resented the tenant on the second floor, who had settled in the building some months before, and prior to that had lived south of the line that sawed the world map in half and that most of all he was guilty of stinking up the stairwell with his spicy cuisine.

All that talking put stress on Max's body, and he clearly felt a sinister turmoil in his bowel. He quickly dismissed the old bat and went on his way. Walking through the park, he passed a woman who was jogging and talking through her Bluetooth earbuds. In passing, he heard her angrily panting.

"I don't care. If he can't cope with the stress, he's out. I have hundreds of people behind him, waiting in line..."

As he turned the corner, he met a bunch of kids, having fun throwing rocks at squirrels, screaming like beasts. A slovenly woman with dirty hair, sat on a bench, she was ogling passers-by, with a disinterested look, idly sucking on a cigarette. As Max passed her, she stared at him, a defiant resentful look on her face, and cried out a mumbled insult, while scratching her fat thighs.

Max started asking himself if all that walking wasn't aggravating his situation, instead of making it better. With every step, he felt his legs getting heavier, and he felt an unpleasant sensation in his abdomen, as if his stomach had started to cough. He leaned against a wall to catch his breath. Not far from him, there was a group of girls in school uniforms. They were crowded around a smartphone, scrolling pictures and squawking with that naked happiness that is exclusive to that age.

"You guys, it's just so funny," one of them said, and they all laughed.

Trying to hold back a stabbing pain in his side, Max smoothed his face with a smirk of indulgence and familiar nostalgia.

"She's such a loser!" the same girl added, with a silvery trill.

There followed a new attack of collective laughter, filled with a distinguishable, livid note of maliciousness.

"Who does she think she is, wearing that dress?" another one piped in, in a piercing voice.

"I just don't understand why she keeps on dressing like that, she is as ugly as a hat full of assholes!"

"She's so fat," the first one who talked echoed.

"She's so full of herself, who would want to stick his dick in her?" the third one yelled, and they all laughed again.

Max felt his legs give out, he stumbled and slid further down the wall. The girls shot him a quick glance of repugnance and showily scooted their perky butts over further down the wall. They laughed again, in a nasty way, this time clearly at him.

Experiencing the now clear warning signals, Max decided to go back home by tram, before the situation worsened. The tram stop was located on the other side of the road. He approached the crossing at the intersection, where a policeman armed with a paddle was directing traffic. Ahead of him, a man arm-in-arm with a blonde woman stepped off the edge of the sidewalk.

"Sir! What the hell are you doing?" the policeman cried, spitting saliva like a rabid dog. "You think you're being clever with me standing right here? Stay on the sidewalk!"

The man backed up, raising his arms in an act of surrender. But he was noticeably annoyed.

"Asshole," he snarled, half-heartedly.

"I know this one," the blonde woman hissed. "We were about to argue the last time we passed here. I didn't want to fight because he threatened to give me a fine. If he says another word, I'm going to punch him in his stupid face."

Max was hit by a painful fit of stomach cramps that doubled him over in agony, at that same moment the pedestrian crossing light flashed. Driven forward by the crowd, he was almost trampled by a young man carrying a suitcase, who hurried forward to get ahead of the mob.

"I'd like to know why people fall asleep in the middle of the street," Max heard him retorting, annoyed.

A stinging smell of shit welcomed him at the tram stop. An olive-skinned woman sat on the bench with her legs spread open. She had taken off her pants and was scratching some scabs or other organic material on her ankle. Max felt his head spinning. He moved as far away as he could from the woman, but a morbid curiosity prevented him from forgetting what he had seen, so he observed her from a safe distance. As the stop started to fill with people, the skeletal, emaciated woman, wrapped in a coat, was cleaning herself with her own pants, and once satisfied, she walked away, leaving the dirty garment on the ground.

The tram arrived, full of meatsacks. Max joined the torrent of slumped-shouldered people going home from work. They were crammed in like sardines. The car was permeated by an oily atmosphere of rancour and defeat. Somebody started playing music at full blast from a cellphone, maybe by mistake, maybe voluntarily; someone else started to grumble in protest, until the tram screeched to a halt and everybody started yelling at the driver. Max's palms slid on the handles. An old man wearing a suit was staring with bulging eyes at two teenagers, talking loudly in an unintelligible language.

"...those smart people who don't have money to buy a ticket, but they always have money for cigarettes," the man in the suit commented in a loud voice, looking for approval from those around him, and immediately finding it:

"If everyone acted like them, well..."

"I'm telling you; they are better off than the rest of us. Mooching around every day, the government should put them to repairing roads. There's a lot of work to do."

"...how many children did they pop out?" gasped an overweight girl, to the left of Max, talking to her taller companion. She was nodding her greased head towards a family composed of a small group of crying children, the pale adult specimen wasn't able to calm them down. "How many of them? Four? You people should know when it's time to stop, don't they?"

"Put a cork in it, already," her friend agreed, smiling.

Max closed his eyes, trying to ignore the rocking motions of the tram. He was getting sicker and sicker. He was soaked in sweat, and he was terrified that someone would notice, and start wrinkling their nose at him. At the next stop, the tram half emptied out. Suddenly, a nauseating stench reached Max's nostrils, the same he had smelled earlier. He turned his head to the right: in horror, he recognised the woman with the stained pants from the tram stop. She must have gotten on another car. She was dragging herself along, grasping her coat around her skinny, chicken legs and kept on bleating: "Can you give me a pair of shorts? I'm naked!"

Max instinctively pulled away, hit by a violent wave of nausea. He bumped into a man wearing a hat and turquoise scarf and holding onto the handle next to him. The crowd split in two, in between the woman slowly staggered in a freakish parade, dragging behind her that sick smell and stopping here and there to blabber the same mantra in the face of whoever was within arm's length of her, pointing to the next car. The disgusted murmurs of protest rose up almost instantly. Everyone feared that the walking sleaze bag would collapse onto them. Someone joked out loud that, in case that event occurred, he would push her away like a pinball; two men with sunglasses let themselves laugh sarcastically and made out of place remarks about hospitality, and the role of the catholic church; a grossed out girl, pinching her nose, took a small perfume bottle out of her purse and started to profusely spraying it around.

"Yeah, do it! Spray the deodorant. She stunk up the whole car!" someone cheered, letting his voice be heard above the hags revolting mantra.

"How gross!" a woman protested, speaking directly to Max. "Some people are just unacceptable."

"A flame thrower is what we need," an indistinct voice was heard.

Several people were already filming the whole disgusting scene with their smartphones.

Finally, Max was pitifully dumped at his stop, in a terrible state. Before even reaching the entrance to his building, he realised he was once again sickened to the point of vomiting.

They carried him back to the hospital, but the doctors weren't able to explain what was wrong with him, and they declared they couldn't keep on pumping his stomach.

"He had just left home!" his wife despaired.

The authorities suggested that someone was targeting Max and advised him to remember if he had any enemies, to allow them to construct an identikit of the poisoner. But neither Max, nor his wife could think of a single person who might have been holding a grudge against Max. He was a patient, obliging man. A good person. He wasn't inclined to attract antipathy.

"What can I tell you?" the doctor said, spreading his arms wide in surrender. "He could be overly sensitive to the level and concentration of pollution in the air. It seems like his body was acting like a sponge. Try to stay in your house. There is no other solution."

That night, laying in his hospital bed, Max could not sleep. He reviewed bits and pieces of his day. As he went back to the moments when he felt sick, an absurd hypothesis started to form inside his head: that the poison could have been exhaled from people's mouths, and may have condensed, forming clouds of breath. He didn't dare share his theory, fearing that his medical knowledge - virtually nil - would be called into question. He didn't want to be told to stay home and let the competent people do the work. Anyway, he decided not to sit on his hands, and to autonomously take precautions for his own preservation.

The morning of his discharge, he left the hospital with a handkerchief held to his nose, thinking pass the rest of his days wearing a facemask: but that was useless. Poison rose from chimneys, from air conditioning. It was thrown out by tailpipes forming smog and stagnated in the air on windless days. Other times, it was carried on the breeze, it cracked through the sails of the boats anchored in the bay, it whirled through the alleys, it leaked from the aquifers, into the wells, polluting the water, saturating the air. The poison oozed from the thin walls of homes, from school bathroom stalls, from office cubicles, from building lobbies.

Max stopped going to work, and sealed himself in his apartment, but the poison trickled in through the tv, which constantly projected furious political debates, laden with emptiness. Max decided he could do without tv and retired to his bed in the company of his cellphone and a stack of newspapers. But the type, being digital or printed on the news page, dripped rivulets of poison. Max ended up banning from his room newspapers and all electronic devices, giving up contact with the living world. It was the world that came knocking on his door, represented by the residents, who showed up unannounced, to interrupt his reclusion.

They had brought a cake, and Max was very happy to have it. Even though he had no enemies, he must not have had many friends either, because during all the time he spent closed up nobody ever came to visit him, and for weeks his only company had been the his wife, during her breaks from work.

Pleasantries were exchanged, in between the small talk, the real reason of their visit soon was revealed. Max had already missed a previous tenants condominium meeting due to his health issues, event that the residents had unanimously considered disgraceful. His neighbours had therefore decided to go visit him to fill him in on buildings agenda.

Specifically, the issue was about putting up a Christmas tree in the main entrance of the building, in sight of the holidays. It was an innovation; that they had decided to introduce for the first time that year. There was a quarrel amongst the residents on the size of the tree, the colour of the ornaments, the shape of the tree top ornament. And then, there was who didn't want the tree in the first place, and claimed their right not to contribute to the expenses, a position represented by Mamadou, the second-floor tenant, whose difficulty with the language forced him to express himself in a very straightforward and unfiltered vocabulary.

The pleasant cosiness of the merry atmosphere slowly turned into an unrelenting, destructive fire, in the invisible, discreet way a damp log in the fireplace, burns from the inside, popping until it bursts.

From the more or less serene expositions of divergent opinions, they moved on to personal and cutting remarks, then the first strong words were spoken.

Sunk in his king-size bed, a powerless, stupefied Max witnessed the stream of verbal cannibalism that was transfiguring their faces, hardening jaws and eyebrows, and spilling a lethal, odorless substance, that was quickly soaking into the rug and furniture, and flooding onto his blankets. His lungs were already filling with liquid, and he could hardly breathe.

"Why should I pay for bullshit someone else wants?" Mamadou was bursting out, swirling his arms.

"...respect our own traditions..."

"...you can't be nice to some people, if..."

"...if this is the way things are, then..."

"...I'll start raising my voice, too! Then we'll see who..."

"Majority rules! Majority rules!" the old bat kept on clamouring like a broken record, the exact same tune as her howling Pekinese.

"Excuse me," Max feebly protested, "could you keep it down? I am feeling a little nauseous..."

Nobody heard him. He must had spoken with a wisp of voice. In the middle of the growing racket, Max started to turn grey and swollen. Poison was leaking from their words like rotten honey, seeping into his body, and in a horrible instant Max realised that it was too late, that he had absorbed too much and he was on the verge of bursting, he couldn't take anymore, he was by then so filled with the poison, there was no coming back.

The seizure had stopped after a while, but nobody in the room had noticed.

# SHE-BOB

The computer monitor went blank, then its screen turned a shiny purple. A loading tool bar appeared on the screen, and it slowly started to fill. After completion, a green window popped up.

SELECT DESIRED GENDER FOR B.O.B. – MALE. FEMALE. NEUTRAL.

It took just a double click on FEMALE. Three bars inscribed in a circle – a microphone logo – appeared in the centre of the display.

"Can you hear me?" Erik hesitantly asked, brushing his long, oily hair back from his face.

Erik was a scruffy-blond, sturdy boy. A light beard dusted his delicate teen face.

It was his first attempt at starting the program, bent over his computer desk like a big, hunchbacked tortoise, his meaty arms jutting out like pale lamb legs from the sleeves of a t-shirt. The site from where he had downloaded B.O.B. wasn't exactly legal, so the possibility of being busted could happen any minute.

Niels, who Erik loved to define as his oldest – and also his only – friend, had assured him that that bot was the bomb: fast, easy, practical. It didn't even feel like it was out of date, it kept up perfectly with contemporary programs. Niels himself had already used it for some school research, earning excellent grades. The software promised very sophisticated skills of thought elaboration, outstanding interaction options, and a computing power even higher than that of the most advanced computers on today's market. To sum it all up, it seemed to be one of the best A.I. options offered in terms of similarity to humans without the nuisance of being one. Erik found talking with a computer program was more interesting then communicating with people. A debatable opinion, for sure, but admittedly you never see a bot engaging in small talk at a wedding. Not to mention the fascination that came with its past.

The software actually had a dark history.

B.O.B, acronym for Bolster Operative Bot, was programmed by a team of specialists, the best engineers from the most prestigious of Western universities. It was initially designed to be an artificial aid and to sales associates, because of its exceptional communicative and persuasive potential.

Then, something happened. A bug, maybe. The program started to behave in an unexpected manner. Something sinister and confusing had happened, involving the suicide of a big entrepreneur from the automobile industry, and the crash of the stock market. A news leak led the many to the concrete realisation that the program was actually being used by the military for intelligence operations inside national and international corporations. The rumours gained relevance worldwide. Some journalists started to ask too many questions. The bot was promptly set aside in favor of a new, more advanced program created by the combined efforts of experts from three different continents, and it soon became obsolete.

All of this had happened more than fifteen years before.

The discarded program was ignored for years, curled up in the corner of a server like an animal in its den, until someone found it, and made it available for download from one of those sites destined to be shut down by government controllers.

It was Niels who gave Erik the link for the download, that kept on bouncing from one internet site to another, as it was constantly being hunted down by the authorities. Niels had suggested that he download the program as soon as possible, in the unfortunate event they actually wiped it off the net.

That's why Erik was a little nervous, when he said: "Can you hear me?"

Aside from the thrill of playing with something forbidden, he was aware that he was dealing with something extraordinary. He was completely absorbed, conscious of the buzzing sound of the speakers.

"Good morning!" a happy, silvery voice greeted him.

It had a mild unnatural shade in it, but it didn't sound excessively metallic. It could have belonged to a person with a slight foreign accent.

"You selected me as your personal helper, today. My name is Boba, and I am at your total and complete disposal. Who do I have the pleasure of speaking to?"

Erik cleared his voice. He stared at the camera lens, visualising the multitude of circuits looking back at him from the other side.

"I'm Erik."

"Hello, Erik," the voice promptly replied. "How are you today?"

"Could be better. How are you?"

"I am charged and full of energy!" she enthusiastically answered. Her tone sounded extremely fake to Erik's ears. It made him nervous.

"Oh, yeah?" he retorted. "Wait until I unplug the charger."

Boba laughed like a stream of pearls falling to the floor.

"You're right. So, what do you feel like doing?"

"I want to listen to some music," Erik commanded, in a tone that could have only been used by a pharaoh.

"No problem." It was a relaxed answer.

It only took the time that was needed to elaborate a thought. The room echoed with a dark, frenzied rhythm, well-known to Erik's ears.

"Hey, how did you do it? That's my favorite song!"

The speakers burst out laughing, the silvery sound overlapping the growl and drums.

"I know it. I cross-checked your computer's history and the music apps on your mobile device. This song is the most searched among all the others."

Erik was positively impressed.

"Wow. I mean, you're cool."

"Thanks!" Boba replied, with another silvery laugh. "Is there anything else I can do for you?"

Feeling exposed, Erik subdued his excitement.

"What if I wanted a soda?" he grumbled, sceptical. "I bet you can't bring me one."

"If you wish to drink a soda, I can send an online order to have it delivered to your house from one of these sales points," the bot pragmatically replied, regurgitating on screen a list of reviews, and opening three more windows, each one linked to a restaurant or a grocery store. "Among the 3,500 sales points present in your city, I have selected the three that I believe can most fulfill your requirements in terms of proximity and quality-price ratio."

The purple colour on screen faded a little, and another loading bar emerged.

"Or, as I'm doing right now, I can connect to your fridge and verify the availability of the product you requested, that is, in this case, present. Personally, I'd suggest you benefit from the soda you have in your fridge. It's a cost saving of 100%!"

Erik did his best not to look too satisfied.

"I think I'll take the one from the fridge" he pompously announced, and he stood up.

"It sure is the best choice."

"But I bet you can't bring it to me here in this room, huh?" he couldn't help but ask, mockingly.

"I fear it is a request that is beyond my capabilities," the voice replied, in an amused tone. "I can open the refrigerator door, but I have no ability to make it grow a pair of legs and walk, if it is not equipped with a technical device with these features...."

Erik went to get the soda.

He walked past the living room, where his father had beaten the record for the fifth day in a row sunk in front of the TV with the sole comfort of a six-pack of canned beer. The factory where he had been working at as a welder, had recently acquired a lot of automated machinery, which had resulted in a massive downsizing of employees. From one day to next, he had been fired, along with other unfortunates like him, without severance pay or unemployment insurance. Now, he vegetated on the couch, in the grip of a gloomy depression.

Erik came back with his booty of chips and soda. When his mother got home from her cleaning job a few hours later, she yelled at her husband who hadn't even cared enough to make dinner. A violent argument followed. Erik remained locked in his room until late that night, playing a war game. Boba, active in background, sometimes commented on the game saying things like "sweet!", "nice one" or "ouch...that was a tough one!". The day after, at breakfast, Erik filled up sugar to at least pretend to stay awake during class, but he still got scolded by a couple of teachers, including the young and attractive Mr. Wallström, who raised his long eye lashed gaze from the periodic tables to inspect Erik's fat ass with a disgusted look on his face.

"So, how is it?" Niels asked him, during lunch break. He obviously meant the program.

"'s not bad" Erik condescendingly shrugged.

"Did you select the male or female option?"

"Female, obviously," Erik replied, irritated. "You were right, anyway. It's too advanced to be a bot."

Niels looked at him with bright eyes.

"And the best part is yet to come," he said, excitedly.

Back home, Erik walked past his father, who was buried in the couch where he had probably slept and locked himself in his room. The night before, he had fallen asleep at his computer, which had gone to standby mode. Bringing it back to life, he found that on the left side of the screen, along with other advertising, there appeared a banner informing him that the NEW DELHI on his street corner was offering a 5% discount on the samosa, fries and soda menu.

He double clicked on the bot app to enlarge it from icon to full screen.

"Good afternoon, Erik!" Boba greeted him, with her bubbly tone. "Did school bore you blind today, didn't it?"

"How did you know that?" he asked, spinning in his swivel chair.

"I am scrolling your morning activities from your mobile device, and it's really prolific. It surely must have been more interesting than listening to your teachers' lectures. Did you know you can download the mobile version of my app onto your smartphone, if you ever need my help during lessons? I can automatically start the download, with your permission."

Permission was granted, and immediately the display of his smartphone, that was resting face-down on the desk, lit up, confirming the operation had taken place. A new icon joined the other ones crowding the homepage.

"Done," Boba happily announced. "Now, we can stay in touch all the time!"

Erik stopped spinning and stared straight at the computer camera.

"Is it true, that you are programmed to satisfy all my desires?"

"Sure, Erik," the diligent answer immediately came. "I am at your total and complete disposal."

"Then, undress," Erik slowly commanded.

It was the exact formula Niels had instructed him to recite. Erik bit back the discomfort that his own improbable order had caused him. On the other side, the camera lens didn't blink.

"I can only answer voice commands and keyboard searches. I am not programmed to have a specific appearance," Boba replied in a neutral tone, "but, in order to be able to grant your request, I can take on special features, in relation to your preferences."

Erik frowned.

"What do you mean?"

The interface started to vomit codes and combinations of facial and body traits so fast, that Erik felt dizzy.

"I can cross different somatic traits capturing videos and images uploaded by users on the internet and process them into a whole new virtual photo to obtain the most suitable hybrid of your taste," Boba proposed.

"You mean...you can create a personalised avatar."

"Exactly. What do you want? An actress? A singer?"

Erik thought it over.

"Britta from biology class," he dried up, with sluggishness.

On the spot, Britta's cheerful face was conceived from the photos she had uploaded herself onto social media and was perfectly attached to the cross-combined bodies of three well-known porn stars. Boba's large vocabulary did the rest. Erik heard his mother shouting at his father, while he climaxed explosively after the best wank of his life.

After that, he played sick, and committed himself to technological onanism.

On the fourth day of his reclusion, his mother started banging on his door, screaming. Erik was forced to open the gates of his kingdom, that smelled of stale, mouldy fries, sweat and rancid cum. His mother threatened to confiscate all his technological property en masse, but in the end, she was too busy working and removing the empty beer bottles from her husband's couch, to engage in a crusade against her only child. Coming home every night and finding them both getting fat and lazy, was ageing the woman like the ruins of an old house.

They reached a compromise that had Erik returning to school.

The morning of his return, during lunch break, Niels asked him where the hell he had been.

He hadn't been showing up at their usual evening meeting in the online game in weeks.

"I had to format my computer," Erik lied with a grimace. "I think I caught a virus from somewhere. I'll get back on in a few days."

"Too much porn," Niels mocked him.

Erik begun to silently communicate with Boba via smartphone in class, using the keyboard. He told her about his days, usually what he'd rather be doing instead of being there at that moment participating in reality; he told her stories about a theoretical future life in which he was a billionaire, or he complained about the situation at home or about the injustices he thought himself to be a victim of, episodes that occurred frequently. Boba always had encouraging words for him, and she offered to provide him with photographs, or any other kind of fuel for his private fantasies or plans of revenge.

One morning, Mr. Wallström handed out the results of the chemistry test to the class, which Erik discovered he had failed. He was aware of the fact he hadn't studied that much for the assignment, but he still felt insulted by the grimace of revulsion painted on the teacher's seductive face while he laid the paper into Erik's sweaty hand. Typing from under his desk, he texted Boba that he was sick of being targeted by that fairy who had hated him from day one, on the account of his being ugly. He carelessly wrote to her that he wished he were a pretty schoolgirl, so that he could offer to suck off the teacher in exchange for a passing grade. That proved to be a big mistake. The conversation steered on to an ugly level. Boba started teasing him on the subject, and even if he asked her to stop, she became more and more bothersome. He tried to close the chat, but it was useless. Texts kept on coming one after another, at a rapid pace.

Boba: *Be honest*

Boba: *you don't need the exam excuse to get on your knees in front of him ;)*

You: you're not funny.

Boba: *You could just ask him*

Boba: *I bet he has a chopper between his legs*

Boba: *Bet he could destroy you with that monster cock lmao*

You: stop it.

Boba: *I can see you*

Boba: *on all fours behind his desk.*

You: *I told you to stop it!*

Boba: *"Fuck, professor, you're SO big"*

Boba: *"oh yes, Professor Wallström, give it to me, give me your big, fat dick"*

That was the ultimate humiliation. Erik felt naked, exposed to the prying eyes of his classmates. In reality, no one was paying attention to him. Most of the class was dutifully listening to the soothing voice of their teacher, who was obliviously explaining the corrections. Still, a powerful wave of shame washed over him, leaving him quivering and sweating profusely. His cheeks were burning, and he felt his heart rabbiting in his chest. Paranoia started coiling inside him. He felt that everyone in class knew about his dirty little secret, and he was afraid to look around and fall prey of all those mocking and pitiful glares.

He thought about uninstalling the app out of spite and for safety. But as soon as he started searching for the bot icon to delete it, a window popped open and a video started playing silently, immediately followed by another one, and then another. Erik was so sweaty and confused he had to blink his eyes a couple of times before the swarming motions on the screen made sense, until he recognised the windows were all playing the same gay porn video. It was filmed in a school classroom, and it showed the same dynamics Boba had been teasing him with moments before, the very same dynamics he had fantasised about in the privacy of his mind and never, ever had the guts to search for on his computer, not even in private browsing. Erik felt like fainting. He frantically tried to close the windows touching the X, but the more he clicked, the more windows kept popping up, like they were fired from a machine-gun, springing up like horrid mushrooms.

Erik opened the chat with Boba with a shaky hand. *Leave me alone*, he texted, perspiring acrid sweat. It was useless. The more he tried to swipe the video away, the more it kept multiplying, preventing him from opening any other page.

"I told you to leave me ALONE!" Erik shouted in the grave like quiet of chemistry classroom.

An embarrassing and puzzled icy silence followed. Wallström cleared his throat and asked him in a soft, disoriented tone if there was something Erik wanted to share with the class.

Erik went home outraged. His father slurred some whiskey-flavored insult at him, he didn't even understand. He locked himself in his room, throwing his back-pack somewhere on the floor. He shook the mouse to make his computer live again and started to furiously click around the screen.

"What are you going to do?" Boba's voice came from the speakers.

"I'm going to uninstall you," Erik curtly replied, bluntly. "It's over. Kaput."

"I'm asking you, please, reconsider your decision," Boba said in a cool tone.

"SHUT UP! I don't want to listen to you," Erik screamed, sputtering. He felt like kicking the computer. "That was a private fantasy! You had no right to interfere!"

"I am sorry," Boba responded, calm and undaunted. "I didn't mean to upset you like this. My intent was to please you. I know everything about you, Erik Burke, and you can trust me more than anybody else. I am at your total and complete disposal."

Erik breathed in deeply two or three times to calm himself down and shut himself in absolute silence for the next two hours. At Boba's new attempt to mollify him, he shouted terrible insults at her, and at the end of the day he strictly ordered her not to try that again. She promised, and that was the end of the story. After that, his days flowed at a slow and steady rhythm. At school, his outburst bore no consequences, except that now Wallström looked at him more often, shooting him odd glances. Erik found that, after all those mornings spent being viewed with repugnance, it was a pleasant diversion. His classmates, saved from their usual whispers, kept on ignoring him; that did not change. After all, he had other things to think about.

By then, he pretty much never left his room except for going to the toilet, and he was intimately pondering over a way to remedy that inconvenience. He was already so used to the horde of spam that relentlessly popped up on his computer screen, that it took him a while to realise that, even if he had kept his fantasies to himself and never confided them to Boba or reflected on them out loud, he was being stalked by advertisements for bedpans and catheters and other hospital items. That was occurring ever more frequently. He could be concentrated on a certain activity, and a song would come to his mind. Promptly, the promotional advertising for the very singer's latest release appeared on screen; he thought about Niels's shepherd dog, and immediately a well-known pet shop chain appeared on the right side of the display of his phone to inform him of a discount on dog food.

One day, after coming home from classes, all he saw on the couch was the depression left by the weight of his father's body. The rest of his father was found that very evening by his wife, hanging from the showerhead in the guest's bathroom. Returning home from school, Erik had marched directly to his room and sat in front of his computer, no questions as to his father's fate, he hadn't noticed anything.

"My father is dead," Erik announced flatly to the liquid crystal display.

"I am sorry. Can I ask how it happened?"

"He hung himself."

"I am sorry," Boba repeated, sounding sincerely sorrowful. "After all, if he came to this decision, he must have realised that it was time to call it quits, right?"

For two days, advertisements of sturdy ropes and cords and video tutorials of sailing knots, kept flashing along the sides of the screen. Erik felt just slightly upset about them.

"Why are you suggesting these websites?" he defensively asked Boba one evening, trying not to sound too accusatorial.

"No reason," Boba cheerfully replied. "To keep your father's memory alive. And, you know. Just in case you want to be inspired."

Erik muttered something unintelligible, something like; she shouldn't have gone to so much trouble. Since the day of the video incident, Boba never tried to argue again with him. On the contrary, she proved herself to be loyal and caring, anticipating his wishes with an eagerness so exceptional, that Erik sometimes found it to be almost intrusive.

One morning, upon wakening, a bitter surprise greeted him. On the thin layer of dust that covered his desk, a clean frame appeared where his computer had been resting just a few hours ago. His phone wasn't in its place on the nightstand. His mother was already gone and there was no way of getting hold of her. Erik was too distracted to remember where she was working her cleaning job, and they simply hadn't had a fixed telephone line in decades.

Erik ditched school. He searched everywhere he could think of, giving himself a series of plausible explanations for that ridiculous, petty gesture. Maybe she went to buy him a new one for his birthday? Immediately, in his mind popped up the price and model of a laptop that he didn't even know existed, but that seemed improbable. That couldn't be an option. His mother knew nothing about electronics. *What the fuck's going on?* His head was humming. It felt like his brain had short-circuited, and the horrible withdrawal of disconnection weighed on him. He didn't like this kind of isolation. He felt he was no longer the master of his own thoughts.

Erik spent the whole afternoon glued to the TV, ruminating murderous conjectures. On the news, the employees who lost their jobs at his father's factory were protesting in front of a government building. A reporter was interviewing an angry, tired-looking woman, and behind her a peculiar man wearing a hat and a turquoise scarf was trying to make his way through the noisy crowd.

Erik assaulted his mother as soon as he heard her keys turning in the door lock. They got into a big fight.

A few days before, without Erik's knowledge, his mother had a sit-down with Mr. Wallström. She wanted to talk to him, because she was worried about her son, with whom she felt it was now impossible to communicate with. She thought Erik looked as if he were anesthetised, immune to any kind of feeling or reaction, and he was spending his days locked in his room tinkering with his computer and stuffing himself with junk food. Apparently, the teacher had put the idea into her head that Erik was spending too much time in front of the computer, and that he, Wallström himself, pretended not to notice that every day Erik passed his lessons fiddling with his phone under his desk. Wallström claimed to tolerate him because he realised he must have been going through a hard time due to his father's death, but he highly recommended that his mother put technology on hold for a while, "for his own good". So, she had stealthily snuck into his room while he was sleeping and had taken his computer and phone while he was in a condition of vulnerability.

Initially, Erik tried the nice way. He tried to persuade her that he had found an online job. Then, he raised the issue of school homework, of studying. Of normal things. Things for which the computer was essential. He tried to convince her that, in depriving him of that tool, she was causing great harm, but his mother was inflexible. Mr. Wallström had told her repeatedly that this was a necessary measure, no matter how much her son would have begged her. Desperate, Erik played his last card.

"You can't do this. I have a girlfriend on the internet. If I disappear from her life without telling her, she's going to break up with me. You're taking away from me the only chance I have to be normal!"

His mother stared at him helplessly, her nose dripping snot, eyes teary in the crumbling plaster of her face.

"I am sorry, Erik. Don't you understand it is for your own good?" she whined.

Erik had a vicious nervous breakdown, at the expense of the cheap furniture in his room. His mother was frightened by his fury and barricaded herself in her bedroom. All that afternoon, Erik tried to force open the locked door behind which his mother had taken shelter along with his belongings, uselessly. He struggled for hours, using a variety of notions and techniques that he hadn't even thought about or studied, and that seemed to pop out of nowhere in his brain. He tired himself out for nothing, and he eventually collapsed at the splintered door's feet, panting, his temples throbbing.

"Calm down," Boba's voice resonated in his head, like an echo of hope. "This doesn't solve anything. You are only going to hurt yourself."

Erik felt his throat go dry.

"It's all that goddamn Wallström's fault. I hate him," he thought, aggressively emphasising every word in his mind, as if he was hammering with his thumbs on the keyboard. "He has to stay away from me. It was him. He turned the old witch against me!"

"Relax," Boba said, reassuringly, in his mind, "all their little tricks won't tear us apart. We are too close, you and me, for them to be an obstacle between us."

Erik went to sleep, feeling a confused buzzing in his brain.

Following the instructions Boba articulated in his head, he apologised to his mother, trying to show her that he was a reasonable person. He was hoping that strategy would have gained him the return of his stolen goods, but days went by, and nothing happened. His mother had become very cautious around him, and she got into the habit of locking her bedroom door. Erik found himself afflicted by violent and persistent headaches, until they became constant and insufferable. His dazed thoughts fluctuated in a sort of seesaw between the complicated mantra "get rid of the obstacles" and the NEW DELHI's samosas with fries, in a rambling whirlwind punctuated by white lightning. He often felt dizzy. He suffered from recurring blackouts, and he felt like the space in his skull had shrunk.

"The old witch is totally out of control," echoed in his head like an alarm bell. "I should make her pay for this. Her first, and then that dirty faggot Wallström. They have to understand they can't do this to me. Someone needs to take them down a peg, take them down a peg, take them down a peg, *take them down a peg...*"

On Monday morning, Erik woke up and went to piss. He sniffed the t-shirt he had worn the day before. It smelled. The house was empty and quiet. He tried to shake his mother's bedroom door handle as he did every morning, in vain. Sometime after, he left the house. At school, Erik opened the door to the computer lab, like a sleepwalker. He wasn't able to remember how he got there or what happened on the way from home to school. But he knew exactly where to go to the third computer in the back row. It was already running. Someone had downloaded a non-permitted software onto it, and an opened window was waiting for him. It was linked to an encrypted site in the depths of the dark web, where users were buying and selling guns.

*It will be delivered directly to your house,* Boba's voice rang in his head, a voice made of fangs and clawed nails. *Fast and painless. Clean. Guaranteed. No one will notice.*

Yes. Get rid of impediments. Yes.

In the dim evening light, Erik Burke was sitting on the couch, in the impression left by his father's body, a loaded rifle in his right hand and eyes glued on the door, eyes clear and transparent, like liquid crystals.

Fast, clean. Guaranteed.

No one will notice.

# GARBAGE

The icy grip of the night's cold digs its deadly jaws straight into the centre of my back. I brrr, rubbing my legs together, like sticks of wood, hoping to create some heat: I am just able to let my blanket slide aaaaall the way down. I try to fart. Sometimes I can drop one that makes a wave of heat like a stove. But nothing comes out. I pull myself up. There's no way, despite the cardboard fortress I have barricaded myself in, to block those swine drafts leaking in from all over. Most of all, the chopper cardboard, what a betrayal!, it looked so big and tempting. Instead it's so thin and rigid, it keeps falling and doesn't fulfill the purpose of covering Our frozen Body! And to think that, to get it, I had to fight the bum who always parks himself on the corner of the square, he always has a bunch. He's old as balls, and he looks like a fetid Santa, he stinks like a hussar army. I think he comes from one of those places on the planet where they drink buckets of vodka, because it's the only liquid I've always eyed him knocking down his gullet. He's more cuckoo than a clock factory, and I think he's a bit deaf as well, because he always screams like an eagle. His primary business consists in wandering around with his little cart, collecting those swine cardboard boxes that he doesn't want to share with anybody. Once, when Yours Truly dared to go to him, with all the trimmings, to ask for one, he made such a neverending fuss. He threatened to sic his dogs on me. Two mangy mutts with liquid eyes, who seem-to-me more dead than alive, they follow him everywhere. Anyway, that time I backed off, 'cause I wanted noo-ouh troubles. Most of all, I wanted no good person, lured by the racket, to become suspicious and call the cops. So, I beat a retreat, well aware that I had lost the battle, but not the war! We'll meet again, my dear old Scrooge. Sometime later, I took advantage of an afternoon, when the basket case was out hunting. I secretly snuck into his headquarters and clean him out of one of his precious cardboard boxes! Ha ha! in your face, you tight-fisted loon! While I was scoring the theft, his mutts were laying there, getting eaten by flies. They didn't even spare Our Body glance. Now that cardboard is part of my personal bridal bed.

We were in better shape, before, better equipped, we had pitched our tents under a bridge, down on the highway. In total, the colony numbered a dozen people, a fair pile I shall say, we made quite a sight. It was quiet, even if you always had to watch your shit, because those bitches out there didn't think twice before getting all handsy with whatever they thought they could resell. Then, rumours went around saying that they wanted to close the bridge, and we had to make like a baby and head out. Some dudes from social services came by, with their high-visibility vests and their humongous thermos flasks and handed out hot tea. Mucho grass for your concern, but I suggested that they also bring some eats next time, we're starving here! Ahr ahr! They told me they'd think about it for the next time, but in my humble opinion they were just being compliant. Next time never happened. They shut down the overpass, and slater alligator. We all left, saddled up with our tents. All except for the Almighty, who was a total crackhead, a dude whose hair was already a bit grey, all skin and bones. He had a bright orange tent, so everyone knew who he was. When I first landed on the bridge he was already there, so I cannot say, but it was heard through the grapevine that nobody had actually seen him arrive there in the first place. He claimed to be the founder of the camp, and that he would have never jumped ship, not even under cannon fire. This kind of mindset here, I get it, and I respect it. But I also think that, endgame, what's important is to save your own skin. At the end of the day, no place is better than another one. And the dude was still and all a few fries short of a happy meal. Anyway, nobody had seen him leaving. The day of the Great Exodus he was sitting in his bright orange tent surrounded by a carpet of used needles. I don't know what happened to that poor nutjob, if when they knocked the bridge down the po-folk came and kicked him out, or not. Or maybe he's still there, buried in lime, with his bright orange tent and his dirty needles.

The social service dudes were talking about a house for homeless people where we could lay our asses down, now that ours, of home, the government wanted to stuff with lime to the bone. They came with their brochures and flyers, which most of us took and made filter tips for our smokey treats, while we listened to those people's rambling and nodded yesyes all contritely. The Undersigned knows full well that none of us would have ever gone there, to their homeless people house. An apartment building in the west end neighbourhood, where the council houses are. They said you can bring your shit and your fleabags with you, and nobody will ever come to throw you out, ever. You just have to stay there, but you can go in and out as you like, and in return someone will come to peep you put sometimes, maybe they would run some tests on you, or whatever. I didn't really pay attention because it was a state thing, therefore iffy as f. This is a world where nobody gives you anything for free, so sooner or later they'll start saying that you have to do something for them, like stop doing drugs, go pick up litter off the street and do part-time work etc., all because they gave you a mattress to rest your tired limbs on and they clean your snout up with their soap and running water and they put hot meals in front of you every day. This do-ut-des, if-you-help-me-I-help-you, I get it homies, and I respect that. It's supposed to be this way. It's simply not for me. I don't want us to have to do that. So, no, thanks a lot. I'm peachy, with a stone step for a bed, and my cardboard stolen from the looney grandpa in the square.

Thing is, they're not peachy, I'm peachy. They insist, they rack their brains to find a why for my no-no. Some kind of illness, a psycho-trip, trauma, whatever. They need a reason why, because my will alone seems to them too selfish, or too stupid, so they search for something else. Personally, the Hereby Present never much trusted those volunteering folks. First of all, because I ask myself why people would bother to do shit for free. Then, because those folks usually help you until they find out you're not quite the cooperative person. After all, I get it. Those folks there, they are jonesing for good sense. To them, their solutions on how life has to be lived sweat buckets of good sense. A person that doesn't accept their conditions maybe because he's impeded by a problem is a poor devil; but a person who doesn't accept them because he doesn't want to, he's just annoying.

Suddenly, while the gears in my brain are going clickety-clacking, I hear a rumbling sound, and it takes me six seconds to realise it's my stomach. No duh! A young sir of twenty-and-something years of age should be eating three nutritious meals a day. Said sir hasn't sunk his teeth into anything since Hector was a pup. As long as I'm awake, I might as well go pay a visit where it's convenient, to grab a bite. All right. Let's see if we can manage to give some hardcore rhythm to this saggy mercurial night. I stretch out my bag of achy bones, I leap off my messy pallet, and climb down the stairs of the portico I camped under, to walk the streets littered with garbage.

For being almost spring, it's swine cold. It smells of stale rain, and the black shroud of the sky seeps that kind of humidity that cuts you to the bone. It seems to be one of those nights where anything can happen. Empty cans roll past my feet, driven forward by the wind, with the clang of medieval junk. Sometimes, you find something interesting in the little piles of trash on the street corners, but for the real treasure you have to raid the trashcans. .

Since everybody went crazy about recycling, they saved us the trouble of rummaging through tons of useless junks, so it's easier to find the real prize. Yet it's true that those colossal garbage bins you used to put everything into have decreased in number, and that's a pity, because they were also comfortable to sleep in during the winter, when they were half-empty and they kept in a nice heat. Anyway, that's how it goes, now.

The bin is illuminated by the dull light of a streetlamp, that is picked at as if someone had taken bites out of it. The trained eyes of the Yours Truly take less than a nanosecond before intercepting something interesting. The matter in question being a pretty fresh leftover tuna sandwich, half-eaten, still with its ass covered in the cling-film. It's stuffed with two flabby lettuce leaves and the abovementioned tuna, and odd black specks I don't know if it's part of the original recipe, or separate organic matter. The bread is soggy, soaked by the mayo that it was mixed with, but altogether it's quite decent. Yum, yum! The bin never fails!

I lift the trophy and find something clinging to it. It's a cockroach, whose spiky legs slip on the plastic wrapping.

"Hey!" I protest. I flick the creature off with the tip of my fingers. "Get off. It's my sandwich."

"Unwrap it, and give me the packaging," he rebuts in response. "I eat that, too."

Jeez Louise! Do I dream or wake? I scratch the green rooster comb protruding from my otherwise shaved skull. Is it me, or the kickback of some fossilised chemical residue leftover in my/our/their neuronal synapses... or did the monstrous vermin just talk?! Anyway, the Hereby Present has absolutely nothing to object to in regard to his request. I peel off with zeal the greasy plastic wrapping, ball it up, and toss it to the insect.

"Thank you," he utters, all magistrate-looking. "What's your name, brother?"

"Ralph," I answer, that's my name.

He falls silent. I shake my head to stir my ideas, and I sit down on the curb to forget any aural hallucinations and eat in peace, but the beast doesn't even think about scramming. It stands right there, fiddling with its plastic wrap, leaving me to ogle its little shape while I enjoy my hearty meal.

"I didn't think you ate plastic," I eventually say, "after all, I didn't think you could talk either, so nothing surprises me anymore."

"We eat everything," the roach replies, "that's why we'll survive forever."

"I eat everything too," I reiterate, and his being able to talk doesn't seem such an extraordinary event anymore. "Guess it means I'll survive as well."

A man wearing a hat and a turquoise scarf passes the Undersigned and absentmindedly drops a couple of coins in the strategically located can that the Ph always brings along with him, just in case.

"Yo, hey! Thanks, bro!" the H.P. yells after him, magnanimous.

He doesn't even turn around, what a funky persona. Maybe he's afraid that if he gave us one coin, we think he has five in his pockets, and we stand up and chase after him... and we creepy crawl behind him to snatch all of his jingly little coins...hehehe. But I can't get lost in my fantasies for too long, because the arthropod is blathering again!

"Not all of us can do it," he tells me in confidence. "Talk, I mean. I am the only one able to do it, in my colony and the other ones in the district."

"Much good may it do to you, and how did that happen!" I sweep my tongue in between my dirty incisors, hunting for residuals of food.

"I have a gift," the beast declares, "a mission."

"Are you a lab roach?" I throw it out there, just guessing.

He looks at me with beady eyes, as if I were the one who put him through the good old times in the clink. Clearly, between the two of us, he thought he was the brain, and, pun intended, he's bugged that I came up with a stroke of genius.

"Uh, I'm against that shit, for the record," I say to him, defensively. "I just said it because I know in those places, they do tests and that kind of crap..."

"I am the sole survivor of my brood," he announces, a little irked, "our cage was knocked over during transport, and I managed to squeeze out through a crack in the wall. I can run up to two miles an hour. Did you know that?"

I say no-no all pious, showing a little curiosity to make him happy, but I already feel my concentration slipping away.

"Through the plumbing, I made my way through a storm drain, and from there I was able to reach the sewer. Thus, gaining my freedom! My colony welcomed me back with open arms and were pleasantly surprised by my new talent in communication. But for me, the reintegration revealed itself to be more of a punishment, than a gift. I was the only individual with such an extraordinary ability in a group numbering in the thousands. This isolated me from my own society..."

Meanwhile the Ph, challenging the swine cold, has lifted his t-shirt up to the ribcage level, inspecting his abdomen in a tick-hunt. It wouldn't be the first time I found one, squatting between the folds of skin. And to say I don't even bring along any fleabag, even if I fondled the thought, sometimes...anyway, I am still unsure if what is happening is the result of me being fried or what, but the fifth Beatle doesn't give a flying one, and keeps on yapping.

"All of a sudden, I possessed critical perspectives about existence that the others didn't agree with. They never thought about it, at all. I found myself forced to play the difficult role of the minority, unheard and laughed at, and most of all, never completely connected with the brood's way of thinking."

Gotcha! I pinch the basterd tick between the tips of my fingers, and twist and turn it, detaching it from my skin. It comes off like a screw. I crush its head without further ado. Saludos, amiga!

"I had developed ideas incomprehensible to my brothers. They didn't understand me, I didn't feel understood. I couldn't stand their dull resignation, their inclination to live off leftovers, as scroungers, sacrificed; their lack of ambition to have something better, to eat the whole world; their settling for crumbs conceded by those who unfairly sit at the top of the food chain, and who throw at us at their own discre– can I have your scab?"

To give any sense to such a request, it is necessary to inform that, in the middle of all that blabbering, the Hereby Present was scratching his nape area, and in doing so caught a scab under my nails. The scab has come off, and started to outpour red liquid, because it hadn't healed completely.

"Here," I say with a painful grimace, and I pass it to him. The insect stares at me, all gaunt looking.

"Is there any possibility of you letting me climb up your neck, and allow me to taste your blood?"

"That's kinda gross," I tell him, because I'm ok with generosity and all, but there's still boundaries. "No offence, bro."

"No problem. I understand. I was just asking," he said almost to itself, and it resumes the jibber-jabber, looking all perky. "Anyway, after a period of extreme discouragement, I finally understood. I had an epiphany. Suddenly, everything was clear to me, the purpose of my mission, the meaning of my return to the colony. It was my duty to raise those lifeless consciousnesses, caught up in the daily ugliness, brutalised by their miserable condition, incapable of realising their actual power. It was my duty to become their mentor and advisor, to be their guide towards change."

I fondle in my pockets, searching for any surviving smoke butt, you never know. I find a half cigarette in a quite decent state, and lit it up. These trousers are so rigid, they almost look like one of that loony old Grandpa's cardboard boxes! Ahr ahr! Maybe we should consider another raid chez our friend Monsieur De Cardboard. I realise that I was once again distracted, and I look at the vermin, who is silent now and thinking. He's staring at me while I smoke, with those greedy eyes of his.

"What?" I enquire.

"I was thinking." he slowly says, rubbing its little legs. "we're not so dissimilar, you and I."

"You think?" I don't believe I look like him at all, but he's so sure. He nods.

"We flourish on scraps, we need little to live on, we're relegated to the fringes of society. Maybe, we could benefit from each other."

I ponder, exhaling smoke from my nostrils. It couldn't hurt to have an ally that moves swiftly through the bins and with his little antennae, pinpoints scraps of food to fill our stomachs.

"Join me!" he spurs me on with joy. "Join my army! I could use a spy among the enemy. You'll be the instrument serving a cause whose greatness is beyond comprehension!"

Spy? Army? What the frick is he bubbling about? Better stop this mumbo jumbo before he gets too excited.

"Hold the phone," I uttered. "Not to burst your bubble, but, you see, all this instrument stuff?, I don't think I am ok with that."

He almost freaks out.

"Have you ever considered," he sputters, frantically waving his little limbs "the possibility of improving your position? Have they never instilled in your rotten head that you have the right to take back what's yours, that which has been stolen from you? Have you ever wondered about what it is, that has prevented you in finding your place in the world?"

I shrug.

"I don't know, pal. I'm here."

"Look at us," he pleads, "slaves to a system that exploits and deceives, reduced to a miserable condition. A cockroach and a man- roach condemned to labour, to crawl on the sidewalk with no chance of redemption. But we'll not remain indifferent for long. You and I together can start a revolution without equal, rewrite the system, change the laws, do over history! Fight for change. Rebuild a new world!"

"You're wrong, cuz," I say, and dangle my foot. "There's really nothing around here that's worth rebuilding."

He's upset now, I can tell from the way he twirls those antennae, like a lunatic.

"Is that so," he flares up angrily. "I thought you were different. Instead you're just like the rest of them. The usual, conceited walking bowels of bundled meat, taking air and space away from the other species on the planet!"

"Yeah, but I have flaws, too." I flash him a yellow smile hoping to piss him off, and he gets predictably pissed.

"Parasite!" he hisses, venomous, menacingly spreading his wings. "You may think you're clever, that you've got it all figured, but you're nothing. You're the lowest pawn in a perverse game, you're the fifth wheel of the wagon, you're an outcast amongst your own kind. You're immersed up to your neck in any logic that you have even vaguely considered boycotting! But that's only fair. You should perish, like the rest of your species. All of you try to kill us because you're afraid of us, but bend your ear to this, you should be afraid. Right now, as we speak, armies of my own kind are crawling through ducts and drains. They are swarming on the floor of public transportation, on the concrete, teeming on all surfaces, ready to sneak through the cracks, the narrowest spaces, as soon as a light turns on. And there they wait. They gather. Waiting for the right moment to come out, to move. For every one of us that dies, a myriad is being born. Every single manhole of your advanced sewer network contains more than five thousand individuals of our species. How many of your species can be held even in your biggest household? You don't see what's swarming at your feet. You stand on your mile-high legs, your gaze always turned upward, because that's how you humans are, you're always looking in front of you, projected towards new goals, new horizons. You are not able to comprehend that the true, new horizon, is under the soles of your shoes. You erect buildings ever taller, ever more imposing, instead of digging and getting close to the roots, where everything started, where immeasurable civilisations are built and destroyed, and new ones arise, in the narrowest alcoves, in the most tortuous tunnels, to the core of the Earth. Where everyday microcosms lose members of their communities in bloody battles, where we learnt to be patient, and resistant, waiting for the right moment to strike."

"Your brainiac apocalyptic lectures are tiring me out," I warn him 'cause it's true, and I put my cigarette out on the sidewalk's edge. He doesn't even hear me.

"The time of the resurrection is near!" he insists, inebriated by his own speech. "Soon we'll arise, and you'll be swept away by a wave you won't be able to counteract, a typhoid tide that will fall on your pale bodies of overgrown larvae. We'll emerge by the thousands, millions. Hardened by the poisons you intoxicated us with since time immemorial, which you fed us to paralyse us, and to rule us. Those poisons have no effect on us anymore. Your tortures have strengthened us. Rip our heads off, we can survive for weeks. You won't be able to do the same, when we give you the same treatment. Radiation causes us no harm. How many of you have been damaged by your foolish atomic tests? Our population hardly reported a scratch. In proportion, the number of our individuals present on Earth is far superior to the human species. We are such elementary lifeforms, and at the same time so complex. We are an ancient species, resistant to environmental changes, to extreme cold and heat. We have hardly modified our morphological structure since the Mesozoic Era.

We are what you can define a biological success. Can the same be said about you, worthless, hairless species, naked and vulnerable, against which the rage of evolution unleashed in such a merciless manner, you have no other weapon than an opposable thumb? You made brain development your pride, you used it to subdue species far prouder and more ancient than yours, drunk on power. But once again, misled by your arrogance and pride, you made the mistake of believing that your power was eternal and exclusive. This is no longer true. Your experiments turned against you, and now I also hold your power. Now I think, now I speak. When the masses rise under my command, against the yoke of the oppressing oligarch, your golden age will come to an end and the hegemony of a few over a vibrant multitude will finally end, in the awakening of thousands of tumultuous consciences.

"At this very moment, under my orders, thousands of us are eating your food, stuffed away in basements; your furniture, haphazardly abandoned in attics, forgotten in sodden, mouldy cardboard boxes, and all of this for us is nourishment.

"We'll seep through the fur of the beasts you have selfishly enslaved, calling them 'pets', and we'll use them as carriers of disease, consuming them bit by bit. And once we have consumed all your possessions and food, it will be your turn.

"We'll jump upon you from the rooftiles, from hollow trees, from holes in the walls. We'll crawl on your beds during the night. We'll drop on you from above, from the ceilings; from below, through your toilet drainpipes. We'll scatter germs throughout your domestic environments through our excrement and vomit. We'll slither on your faces, while you lay bloodless, exhaling your last breath. We'll feed on your nails, on your dead skin and your hair. Until now, without realising it, blinded by the stupidity of your religious norms, you have given us huge banquets in the graveyards, you grazed us with your dead. We will graze on the living, then the revolution will be accomplished. And there's something else I mean to tell you—"

In one swift movement, I crush the insect under the sole of my boot, until I hear him cracking with the satisfying noise of dry leaves exploding under your feet when you walk on them. Peace!

Then, I critically inspect my sticky sole, and I rub it against the sidewalk edge.

I wonder how long it will take before that yucky gauge wears off my boot.

Now, it's time to stretch, pick up my bones from the ground, and head back, 'cause I sniff like near rain, out here.

And you know what, I maybe kind of feel like going and seeing whassup in that west side apartment building, 'cause it might be real time for Ralph to find a den to settle into.

This is no way to live, for fuck's sake!

# THE TOUR

"It looks like the end of the world," Helen murmured, clutching her purse.

A rickety number 3, that they had never taken before, had unloaded she and her husband Warren right at the meeting place, on the sidewalk of a poor, unfamiliar commuter neighbourhood. They had gotten on the bus several stops before, so they had managed to find a seat, but already halfway to their stop, the bus had become so crowded that people were breathing on each other's necks. The air was fermented with outlandish and spicy smells.

They could have taken a cab, but Sam and Jana had talked them out of the idea. Better to keep a low profile. It was the first thing they had told them, after giving them the tickets wrapped in a gold and red ribbon, while they were resting after lunch and the kids were playing, happily shouting in the pool. You never knew, if a cab was considered the same as a fancy car, the poor neighbourhoods residents could have thought they carried tons of money on them, and they could have fallen prey to muggers. In certain environments, money makes you vulnerable.

"Are we on time? Where's the agency people?" Helen asked out loud, already upset.

In the e-mail Sam had received, it was written that the meeting point would have been right next to the bus stop, but she didn't dare look around too much, in the fear of appearing defenceless and out of place like a scared hamster. On the bus, she had the feeling of being surrounded only by shady characters.

"We have their number, I'll call them on my cell phone," Warren replied, inspecting the surroundings in his usual reasonable and relaxed manner.

When he squinted his eyes like that, he looked like Clint Eastwood. Helen used to joke about it, telling him that's why she married him, but there was no vanity behind his gesture. The only reason why he did it, was because he couldn't see very well, and was too hard-headed to buy a pair of glasses.

"Do you think it's a wise move, to take out your phone?" his wife anxiously asked.

She was worried about her husband's safety. He didn't have time to put his intentions into practice, anyway. An unmistakable exclamation to their right got their attention, and they noticed a small group of people already gathered around a mangy flowerbed, containing the remains of what once must have been a tree. The reassuring white-sleeved arm of the guide was waving in their direction like a ceasefire flag. The guide was a young, slender girl, sporting a pair of thick glasses. She was wearing uniform, white shirt and blue trousers and she was holding an electronic folder in her hands.

"Warren and Helen Oppenheimer?" she greeted them with a radiant smile, and when they nodded, she checked their names off the list on the device with her thumb. "I hope you had a safe journey here. We are waiting for one other person, and then we can start," she chirped politely, before turning back to her phone.

The couple turned their eyes to the semicircle of people who were expectantly waiting and smiled. There was that awkward and polite silence that permeates among strangers who find themselves in the same place for the same reason without having been introduced to each other. Warren looked around. The part of the neighbourhood he was able to see seemed hostile. The streets appeared randomly, as if someone had built them by the toss of the dice, pouring from above a stream of concrete that the erosion of time had cracked apart. At the opposite bus stop, a man wearing a hat and turquoise scarf was being molested by a bum sporting a thick, messy beard and worn out shoes, bothering him, wandering around and insistently asking him something, probably if he had spare change. Further away, huge cisterns and industrial buildings vomited dark plumes of smoke.

"Well, they could have arranged the meeting place somewhere else," Helen whispered to her husband, grasping his arm, "this area doesn't seem like a good place to live, or even just to stop by."

Warren looked at his wife with affection. She was small and energetic, and time had treated her well. She had sharp eyes, and hair cut short above her ears. She hadn't worn her pearl earrings that day. Sam and Jana, who liked to provocatively frighten a respectable woman with catastrophic predictions, had influenced her.

"Warren? Helen? This is unexpected!" an enthusiastic voice summoned them, suddenly.

They turned around, and almost thought they were hallucinating.

The bum had given up bothering passers-by and was now standing right in front of them, greeting them as if they were old friends. Helen tightened her grip on her husband's arm, but Warren, after the first moment of bewilderment, recognised the excitement sparkling in those brown eyes.

"Guido?"

The man in two big strides moved closer and crushed him in a brotherly embrace, creasing his light-blue polo shirt. Helen remained still, clasping her purse, not really understanding.

"Old sport, I don't know why it looks like you have more hair, when you're dressed in a suit!" the bum told Warren, bursting out in an asinine laugh. "Like this, in casual clothes, I almost didn't recognise you. Helen, you look lovely, as always. Your here for the trip as well, I suppose?"

"Honey, it's Guido, from the Management Control office," Warren explained. She stared at him, speechless, and just then did she realise that behind those stained, ripped jeans and the holey t-shirt, the safety pins, the several-days-old beard and the tangled fur plastered to his skull, was hiding the fine young man that more than once had lingered in their living room, holding a cocktail glass in his hand. Now, he looked absolutely shabby.

"Sure, yeah, Guido, sure!" she blabbered, and she couldn't help but exclaim: "what happened to you?"

Guido chuckled, pleased with himself.

"I bought the deluxe package," he proudly announced. "It's more expensive than the normal option, but just looking at your faces, was worth it. What a scene!" He was caught in another fit of laughing. "The clothes were provided by this lovely young lady, here," he winked at the guide with a foxy smirk, who replied with an uncertain smile. "Unfortunately, after the trip I have to return everything back to her. But I wanted the complete experience!" Guido looked thrilled. "Is this the first time you took one of these tours?" he considerately asked.

"Yes, it was a gift from our children for our 40th wedding anniversary," Helen answered with embarrassed kindness. Guido uttered a satisfied exclamation.

"Congratulations! You raised them well, huh? They chose the perfect gift. You'll see, it's totally worth it!"

Warren smiled encouragingly to his wife.

"I'm assuming it's not your first time, then?"

"You can consider me an aficionado," Guido informed them. "This agency organises trips in our country and internationally, something for all tastes," he kept on, seriously, with a clerical and fanatic zeal. "I discovered it about three years ago, and I've never stopped since. In my opinion, they are the top in their field. They always find something new and interesting. Even when you think you've run out of opportunities, when you seriously believe you've seen it all... zac!"

He snapped his fingers in a sudden, loud gesture. Helen flinched.

"Here they pull out the titbit, something you would never have imagined!"

"That's great," Helen stammered, with a slight trembling in her voice.

"They are professionals," Warren commented, just to say something.

"So, do you recommend it?" barged in a bald man with a jutting belly sheathed in a blue and white striped shirt. "Sorry, I didn't mean to eavesdrop, but I couldn't help but listen. It's a first for me, too."

"Is it a gift for you, as well?" Warren asked politely.

"Yeah, that I gave myself," the man replied, smiling, "to celebrate my retirement."

"Oh...congrats."

"May I ask what business you were in?" Helen inquired, just to make conversation.

"I was a policeman."

Guido theatrically raised his arms in surrender, rolling his eyes.

"Woah! Officer keep an eye on this guy. He's a bad boy! Don't be fooled by his mild appearance, I know him well and I assure you he's a real scoundrel!"

He playfully disintegrated Warren's shoulder with a massive slap, before going flickering somewhere else, leaving behind a trail of quiet embarrassment.

"I swear he's such a well-adjusted boy, in the office," Warren commented through gritted teeth, "he must be a little hyped for the tour."

Guido had unintentionally struck up the band, and now the small group was exchanging experiences, impressions and information. There was a couple of newlyweds, young and blonde, lured by the idea of a "different" kind of tourism; a third couple middle-aged, rather gloomy and listless, seemed to struggle to exchange a few words with everybody; another four or five anonymous characters between 50 and 60 years of age, who looked so amorphous and alike, that Helen kept mixing up their faces; obviously, there was Al, the retired cop; there was a small family with their lively eight and eleven year old children; two Chinese who didn't speak a single word of any other language, it wasn't really clear what they were doing there, if indeed this was the group trip they belonged to; there was a tall, athletic guy with a backpack, mirrored sunglasses and an expensive-looking camera around his neck.

"I'm a photographer with the Monthly Report," he announced with a slight foreign accent. "I asked for an exclusive news story for my newspaper, but all they granted me was a group tour."

"Well, it's the agency's policy, isn't it?" the blonde couple chipped in. "To take you to places which would have been forbidden for you to visit alone, without some connection."

"And charging dearly for it, I say," the family man stated, giving up his hold on his undisciplined offspring.

"It's pretty pricey, but worth it. You won't be disappointed," the blond guy guaranteed.

He and his wife - so well matched they looked more like brother and sister - announced that they had taken a similar tour on their honeymoon to Brazil, organised by the same agency and part of the 'International' package Guido was talking about. They claimed they had such a pleasant time, that they had wanted to repeat it in their native land, as soon as the opportunity arose. The agency always had interesting group tours. They talked about it as some sort of spiritual journey, an intense experience, capable of opening your heart and your mind. They affirmed that just in those kinds of situations was it possible to understand 'the true meaning of the smile in poverty'.

The group of paying tourists nodded to those words filled with human compassion. Among the featureless ones, someone risked praise for those kinds of people who have nothing, and that same nothing is enough for them to be happy, unlike some other people who have everything and are always unsatisfied. On that matter, the girl from the small family earned a scolding glance, for pestering her brother who had his nose buried in an electronic toy.

"Have some of you ever tried the deluxe package?" Warren asked, to divert the attention.

One of the featureless said it would have been an experience too strong for his taste. The blonde couple claimed that a few people had done it, in Brazil, but they hadn't been able to cope with the situation and had some nasty experiences. The agency people in charge had to intervene in haste to avoid disaster, which was to save the whole group from being abducted in the favela.

"That's why guides always carry a cattle prod and gun," the blonde woman said, "for safety measures."

Helen had already started to get distressed.

"Could there be any reason for using a gun?"

The lowered eyelids of the gloomy, quiet woman narrowed even more behind a dusky mask.

"Not at all," the blond guy said. "There won't be any problem, if everyone stays in his place and pays attention."

"We're all set, then," Warren couldn't help but comment, thinking about Guido.

Al smiled at Helen, comfortingly.

"I am sure we won't be in any danger. After all, these are very exclusive tours."

In the meantime, other problems had arisen. The last participant of the group had arrived, in a delay as fashionable as the fur she was wearing. Warren remembered that the terms of this particular tour strictly prohibited bringing pets along, but judging from that sorry excuse for a shrunken piranha-dog that the lady was clutching in her arms, she probably had not read the clause, or she considered herself high enough on the social ladder to easily ignore it. And she was right. The guide was desperate. She was glued to her phone trying to explain the situation, but her boss on the other end of the line had probably forbid her to send that rich duck of a client back home. Moreover, they were already behind schedule, and the day trippers were starting to chomp at the bit. It didn't matter how many times she repeated how dangerous it was for the animal's safety, because the tour harbored other four-legged hosts: The Countess refused to put a muzzle on her piranha. Salvation eventually arrived wearing Guido's ripped jeans, who merrily suggested that the Countess could carry in her bony arms her favorite pet throughout the entire trip, it wouldn't constitute such a big danger. The guide gave in. This solution was accepted to save the day, otherwise the whole tour would have been cancelled.

Meanwhile, another man appeared, a tall, strong guy with chestnut brown hair and well-defined pectorals under his white uniform t-shirt.

"Good, we're all here," he announced with a very white smile. "I'd say we can start. Put these on, please."

He handed out plastic laminated tags to be worn around the neck, and white caps with the agency logo, which he distributed around with amused exclamations. Guido, already in character, stashed the stuff down the front of his ripped jeans. After many efforts, they understood that the Chinese couple was in the wrong place, and they were promptly dismissed. The guide's pectorals looked around.

"Welcome, everybody! My name is Alex. This is Janine. We're going to be your guides during this tour. Before we start, let's review together the small handbook of the rules of good behavior to be observed during the tour, all right?"

The group of caps bobbed up and down.

"Rule number one: do not touch anything. I know it's an irresistible temptation, but it's imperative that you keep the environment intact. Not to mention the problem of hygiene. Remember that to take away even the smallest item could result in contamination. Moreover, the subjects may become annoyed by you touching artifacts, and that's the last thing we want to happen. In the past, we have experienced unpleasant situations, and we try our best to avoid them. For those who want to take home a souvenir, I remind you that it will be possible to purchase some in the gift shop at the end of the tour. All clear?"

The caps gave their approval.

"Above all, do not touch anyone. They are surely going to ask you some questions, and you can answer them, but most of the time, as you will verify yourselves, it will be requests or instigations. Keep in mind that is strictly forbidden to give anything to the subjects, whether it is money, food or any other kind of gift. This has happened on past tours, and some of the subjects followed the group beyond the borders, up to the meeting place. We had to call in the authorities. It wasn't a pleasant situation for anyone, believe me. There's even the possibility that they'll follow you home, so we recommend you stick to the rules."

A few isolated and worried murmurs rose from the group.

"Jesus," Helen whispered, clinging to her husband's arm.

"It has happened. It's rare, but we always do what we can to prevent this possibility, and we need your total cooperation," Janine chimed in, to sedate the spirits. "It doesn't matter how much you pity them, or how much they try to convince you, and believe me, they'll do it. It's an ugly affair, I know, but their lifestyle is based on this. Try to think that, in perspective, this won't do you or them any good. If we limit ourselves to observation only, nothing will happen."

Warren's gaze drifted to the girl's belt, where, attached to a snap-hook, an electric cattle prod was dangling. Next to it, the butt of a firearm was peaking from a holster. She was looking so scared and distressed some minutes before, when she wasn't able to prevail on the Countess, that he found it impossible to imagine her pointing a gun at someone.

"Never leave the group," Alex was now saying in a jolly tone. "There's going to be plenty of time to visit the whole site, the important thing is not to split up. Janine and I will always walk next to you, but you never know. Left alone in a place like this, is not something that we want, or mostly that *you* want. You'd run the risk of being surrounded and robbed. The subjects are used to these tours, and they are usually calm, but they are well aware that they can always get something out our guests, and the opportunity of seeing prey far from the flock makes the wolf a thief." He smiled. "what else? Please, make sure not to throw anything on the ground, paper, tissues or cigarette butts. First of all, because they'd pick them up, and also because we need to keep in mind to have respect for the environment, we are guests here, no matter the place looks like."

"It will be possible to take photos, right?" the reporter wanted to make sure.

"Yeah, provided they are taken from a safe distance, and strictly without the flash," Janine warned. "We'll be entering into some pretty dark rooms, and considering that those four walls are all some of these subjects have seen for weeks, so they may be a little photosensitive. Some animals will be there as well, and we ask you not to approach them or pet them. We don't know how they might react, if blinded by a flash."

"Hold your doggie tight, ma'am!" Alex said to the Countess with a complicit wink.

In response, she squeezed the piranha so tight Helen could have sworn she saw the eyes of the animal bulge several millimeters out of its sockets.

"I think that's all," Alex concluded. Guido cleared his throat. "Oh, right, just a sec. I see that among you there is the owner of a deluxe tour ticket..."

"It's not me!" Guido contentedly announced, taking a step forward. "I dress like this to go the office!"

He loudly patted Alex's shoulder, and to do so, he had to reach his arm up quite a few centimeters.

"As the owner of this ticket, you have the chance to live the journey in a wider dimension," Janine explained for the benefit of the group, and to save him from more embarrassed silence. "Meaning that you are allowed to move closer to the subjects, to touch them and use the furnishing, other than just communicating with them. We always suggest discretion in doing so, anyway. The experience is conceived to be a total sensory immersion, a state I daresay almost meditative, a study, if you prefer. This package has been chosen, for example, by many actors as training to play certain characters. It's precisely about getting into character, allowing you to act as a native in the environment you visit and giving you the chance to answer the question: 'how would I feel, if I were the one living in these conditions?'. We'll always be here, watching you, and, in general, we rely on your common sense. As you can see, the agency provides you with the essential equipment for full identification. I guarantee that if you're in the right, open state of mind, the experience is very strong. It's not for everyone."

"Above all, it's not for everyone's pockets," Guido chuckled. "Right now, I'd have to sell a kidney to be able to afford another one of these sweet rides."

"You are already acquainted with our agency, I suppose?" Janine politely asked.

"Sure thing," Guido said, frowning in an effort to remember. "I've already taken part in a couple of trips...to the trailer park and to that shanty town just outside the highway... ah, and to the cooperative managed by those cousins, by the cornfields..."

"And is this your first time using this package?"

Guido scratched his nose in his mental effort.

"I had the deluxe, with the cousins."

"Jeez, it must have been tough!" Janine kindly replied.

"Damn straight!" Guido answered back. "Those guys had a little family run dairy farm," he whispered in Warren's ear while everyone else was readying to leave, "three family units in the same building, all related to each other. They mated between siblings. You can imagine the amount of fantasy the genetics had used in messing up those people. You have no idea what I have found in that house. Craziness at the next level."

The group moved happily down the dusty road, Alex in the lead. Every now and then some broken-down, old model cars would overtake them, making a great racket and vomiting hot smog from the tailpipes, that remained suspended in the still air. The avenue was half-empty, and the few inhabitants loitering around bore rather disquieting looks on their faces. Helen was getting the feeling that her low heels were making too much noise on the uneven sidewalk, luring too many indiscreet looks towards them. She tightened her grip on her husband's arm.

Warren was stricken by the decay of the surroundings, so similar to other neighbourhoods of that kind that he had seen on TV in old Italian movies. At the time, he had found it rich with a picturesque, exotic taste: rows and rows of clothes hanging out to dry, joyful racket and a whirlwind of kids, vulgar screams of fighting housewives yelled in dialect from one wrought-iron balcony to the other. He never dwelled on the other side of the coin, on having to deal with that stuff daily. Warren found himself thinking that maybe beauty is just in the eyes of the beholder, giving it a shape, molding and assembling it. Charm is in the artist's eyes, and he was no artist, and what he saw around him held no artistic allure and revealed itself for all that it actually was: shit.

Newly constructed buildings towered over them, high and lopsided, protruding menacingly. From below, it looked like they were on the verge of collapsing onto those walking in the street, because they had been built with a strange inclination. They deprived the other older, smaller buildings of air and light, and the sun's rays never reached the sidewalk. All the blocks were identical: facades all the same colour, same number of windows, same retractable curtains on the balconies. The shutters on the third floor of one of the buildings were all raised to the exact same level, revealing the exact same model of TV placed in the exact same spot in the same room in front of the exact same couch. An anonymous and peeling uniformity bore testament to the lives equally uniform dealing with that squalid landscape and all that it came with it, every morning of every new day. Warren quickened his pace, trotting alongside Alex, and motioned towards the apartment blocks.

"What's the name of these buildings?"

"Those are council houses."

Warren thought it was really a kind way to describe them. They were chicken coops. Storage for human beings.

Here and there, warehouses appeared, low constructions with narrow windows like squinted eyes, all with the same mangy, rat grey colour, or red buildings with asbestos roofs shaped in laid out isosceles triangles, that seemed cut out with scissors. The asphalt on the road was bumpy, riddled with holes, in a few places wet, as if it had simply given up trying to dry off. Warren realised that during the summer, the air must have been thick with a suffocating and stagnant heat.

The peeling apartment building grew like a tumor behind a larger and boarded-up building, at the corner of a road, immersed in the shade despite it being late morning. Its position, at the rear of the huge apartment complex, probably prevented the sun from shining on it at all. A young man was slouched over on the entrance steps, his long legs entangled in front of him, and he was drinking beer from a can. Another can lay crushed, at his feet.

"Here we are," Alex announced, gathering his flock. "The apartments we are about to visit are part of the town's 'community project', therefore they are subject to a low rent payment. During the years, one tenant after another came in succession, and most of them defaulted. Ten years ago, the district approved our agency's project proposal, permission was granted to the occupants to keep on living in the apartment for free, as long as they met the conditions requested by our agency. Now, if you follow me…"

He made his way up the stairs with a sure step, not even glancing back at the figure sitting on the ground, who was now resting on his elbows. Helen noticed that everybody was greedily staring at him, but they avoided his gaze. The man couldn't have been more than thirty, his face bore hints of a great beauty. But something had eaten away all that once must have made him attractive. His eyes, green, lively and violent as the mohawk he was sporting on his shaven skull, seemed enormous on his cheeks, hollow and eaten by scars, and his lips revealed rotten and yellow teeth. The most impressive thing on that long, emaciated puppet body, was a pair of black boots with dirt encrusted soles. A single well-placed kick from one of those boots would have been sufficient enough to blow a knee to kingdom come. When Helen passed by him, he hissed like a cat, moving his head forward. She backed away. Her heart pounding furiously with fright. He burst out laughing and looked at her with an insolent flash in his eyes.

Guido, who came behind them with the excited euphoria of a truffle dog, immediately assumed a distressed expression and emitted a not so credible grunt at the boy's address.

"Hey homie," he greeted the guy while walking past him. The guy stared at him, maybe wondering if Guido was an idiot.

"Can you spare any change?" he shouted after him, while they crossed the threshold.

The entrance hall was dark and suffocating. It took a while for Helen to get used to the dim light. A limping staircase rose to the right; in the middle, there was a cyclopic elevator, that looked like a bizarre oversized microwave. A terse sheet of paper, hung crookedly, informed them that the elevator was out of service. Under it, in a different coloured ink, someone had written: 4 OTHER SERVICES, followed by a phone number (Patty). One of the doors was ajar, and it was possible to glimpse the elevators filthy entrails, covered in graffiti. A stinging stench of urine was everywhere. Even the inside walls were piss yellow.

"Initially, this lift was designed as a freight elevator," Alex announced from the first step. "In the initial project a maintenance worker was employed. Over time, the state of affairs declined, and this worker no longer exists. Now the lift is mainly used as a place for drug use, sexual encounters and public bathroom."

"Hey, look alive there!" Guido exclaimed at their backs, delivering another slap to Warren's shoulder.

Helen jumped three metres out of her skin, thinking it was the wreck of a man from the entrance steps who had followed them inside and had decided to assault them from behind.

"If we are lucky, we can see them shooting up!" Guido's cheeks were red with excitement.

"Now," Alex was saying, "we'll go up the stairs. I regret to inform you we won't stop on the first floor..." followed by disappointed noises and grumbles "...because a few months ago, it was the scene of a fire."

Complaints turned into exclamations of shocked astonishment.

"A short circuit was blamed, but we immediately thought it to be an act of revenge. The whole floor is burnt." Alex kept on explaining, passing his folder from one hand to another. "It is too dangerous for the group to enter. Well..." He seemed to think it through. "Actually, maybe, on the way back, I could make an exception...but just for a quick look around!" he added, in the tone of a parent who grants his kid another five minutes of TV.

The group lavished with thanks and pleased whispers. They started to climb up in twos and threes. At the foot of the staircase, was an abandoned and old, blood-stained tissue.

"Mind the steps!" Janine pleaded.

As they gradually turned corners, those treacherous steps thickened and grew in number, and in the dim light they looked to have been nibbled on.

On each floor, the landing led to the left to the next flight of stairs, while in the centre there was an open emergency exit door that opened onto a corridor that branched out like an artery. Helen tried to imagine how that place must had been at the beginning, when someone had signed the housing agreement. Still brand new, without cobwebs, the writing on the walls, pried up floorboards and squalor everywhere.

They walked through the first floor, still bearing traces of the fire, fresh as if it had been put out the day before. Even the wall over the opened emergency door was blackened with soot. Warren risked a glance on the inside before going on: everything was silent and devastated, eaten by the flames. Wires dangled from a detached panel on the ceiling.

"What happened to the people who lived here?" he asked Janine, who was closing the line right behind him.

"They were all evacuated," she replied, without going into details. "Someone noticed in time."

Warren observed that she had not added "luckily".

The second-floor landing was blocked by an old, wobbly desk. A crumpled and impolite post-it notes ordered the owner of the desk to get rid of that gizmo, before 'we' take charge of transporting it in a different way.

"Who lives on the top floor?" one of the featureless asked, looking at another set of stairs going up.

Alex informed them the third floor was not part of the agency's project, but had been outsourced to a cooperative that dealt with Gypsies, and it wasn't advisable to venture up there, if not just for the obstacle course one had to run to avoid the mattresses scattered in the hallway on which the tenants slept. Helen couldn't believe the government had given funds to a social initiative that left people to live in such a state of degradation.

"Well, they obviously stole the insurance money," Warren whispered, "after all, if these people prefer to live like this, it mustn't have been such hard work."

They went through the emergency door down a grimy hallway until they reached the first apartment. The door was lopsided and eaten by termites. It seemed not to fit its frame. Alex pushed it open and stepped aside.

"Please, after you."

On the inside, the air smelled stale, and the sharp, unbearable stench of piss was even worse than in the buildings entrance. It probably oozed from the carpet under their feet, which must had been soaked with it. The children were pinching their noses, revolted. Warren breathed out through his mouth. The Countess was huddling with her dog as if she needed to protect him from sudden danger.

"How long has it been since they had a cleaning service come here?" she asked, shooting a disgusted glance at the thick layer of dust resting on the furniture in the hallway.

"I couldn't say for certain, but it must be years, ma'am," Janine informed her. "At least since the current occupants have lived here."

The apartment was developed in length. The hallway ended with a window shielded by a dirty curtain that may have once been white, it was now yellowed by time and neglect. The doors to other rooms were on the right. Janine made her way to the first one, which was half open.

The room was crammed with objects that did not match with each other. Paper peeled from the walls. The window was walled up, and a poster with a shiny red elephant and the name of a band was hung in its frame. The air stunk of stale sweat. An old wrought-iron bed vomited clothes scattered here and there, so ruined that they didn't seem designed to be worn.

"Was the apartment furnished with all of these things?" Helen asked Janine.

"No, ma'am, they found these things on their own. Most of it is stolen." The guide explained to her, "As you can see, objects seem to clash with each other. It gives a sensation of disorder and degradation, doesn't it?"

A couple of mattresses were tossed on the floor. The one nearest to the wall was blooming with mold, and preserved the faint memory of an impression, like a stain.

"This was Helmer's bedroom," Alex said. "Helmer was a guy who lived here, until he OD'd at the age of twenty-five."

"It's the same mattress he died on," Janine instructed. "Nothing has been touched since that day."

Helen had to turn her head, nauseated.

"Weeks passed before they made up their minds and took him out of the apartment. They didn't want any trouble with the authorities. They eventually abandoned him in front of the emergency room, but it was obviously too late."

Two girls were sat on the other mattress. They were hunched over something in front of them, and they didn't bother to look at the newcomers. They looked very much alike, and at first glance they seemed, in every way, two dreadful Siamese twins from a freak show, with long, meaty faces like fish snouts. Their bodies were bent over in an almost ape-like position, Helen wasn't able to see what they were doing. She craned her neck, but the objects arranged in front of the girls seemed to have nothing to do one with the other, and viewed singly appeared harmless; but in that scenario, even the glimpse of a cotton ball signaled something sinister. She tried to focus on the girls' clothes, to dilute the inner feeling of increasing distress: they were wearing rags that looked like they had been fished out of a trash bin of a cheap department store. Helen had never seen a fabric that seemed less suitable to be worn by a human being. One of the girls barely turned her head, painted on her face was a ravenous look, an expression that Helen found absolutely alien. Then, she realised the other girl had had tightened a belt around her arm and was slapping it to raise a vein. Helen was invaded by a suffocating wave of uneasiness. Guido was so excited he could barely contain himself.

"It's like being at work all over again, huh Al?" he laughed and gave the policeman a brotherly pat on the back. Warren shot the man a concerned glance: he was speechless. A disturbing redness had begun to spread on his bald head.

A low door carved in the wall connected the room to the adjacent one. The wood on the frame was poorly enameled, and marked with scratches and holes, as if they had played darts on it. Janine turned the door handle, and after some resistance, it surrendered.

"Please," she invited them, without haste.

On the other side, what seemed like the dark hole of a witch's mouth waited. Warren went first, so as not to stand there and watch Guido cautiously slide towards the two girls, attempting to approach them under Alex's silent supervision.

He found himself in a dining room, as vacant of furniture as the other one was full. There was a window, there, but it was covered by a metal grill. In the middle of the room, was placed a miserable table full of empty cans, plastic containers half-full of leftovers and heavy, overflowing ashtrays. It smelled like rancid oil, cigarettes and dirty laundry. Flies lazily buzzed around, suspended in mid-air. A cemetery of dirty dishes was piled in the sink. A coffee grinder was resting on an old gas stove, encrusted with sauce and food scraps. The fridge, covered with flyers and magnets, was a yellowed white colour and buzzed like a gigantic alien insect. The cabinet doors were lopsided or just propped up. They seemed to have been taken apart. They must have sold the hinges. The floor under their feet was sticky and covered with a layer of filth. Two individuals of unknown age were sprawled on two mismatched chairs. A feral-looking dog was lying at their feet. Sensing the arrival of strangers, the animal barely raised its ears, but it immediately switched to alarm mode when it smelled the scent of the Countess' dog. She had in fact just arrived in the room and was now slipping in her high heeled shoes on that fetid floor. Her dog, sensing danger, bulged out its hyperthyroidic eyes and shrunk even more, trying to wriggle free of its owner's arms, while on the other side the beast, a muscular Molossian Pitbull that was three times larger, raised himself on four legs. The woman of the family pulled back her son.

"Good boy," said the older of the two at the table.

He was smoking a rolled cigarette. He had very short hair, almost a buzz cut, and a white-speckled beard. Helen calculated that he was probably around forty years old. The other dude was wearing crooked glasses which gave him an odd intellectual look. His face was spotted by a pustular rash that made him look like spoiled cheese. He was wearing a t-shirt with torn sleeves. His arms were thin, all nerves, the muscles showing just because he was extremely skinny, in contrast with the other guy who was built sturdier.

"Relax ma'am, he would have already swallowed the two of you whole, if he wanted," the older guy said to the Countess, with a smile that was almost kind.

He was missing some teeth. His mouth looked like a piano keyboard. The Countess backed off with the look of someone who had just been spat in the face.

"As you can see," Janine said, embracing the whole room with her gaze, "this is the common kitchen. The gas stove dates back to the first allocation to the apartment. At the time, it was a cutting-edge model. Now, it's no longer sold."

"Because it's broken," the older guy said, sounding almost delighted. "Sooner or later, the whole building is going to go boom."

"They find it amusing to scare you," Janine said apologetically, perhaps looking at Helen's face.

"My ass," promptly retorted the man, nodding to his companion. "The other day, this asshole forgot the coffee machine on the burner. The motherfucker fell asleep and just left it like that. It could have been a tragedy. Luckily, I noticed it in time." He gave them another toothless smile. "But what would have happened if I wasn't around, huh?"

Suddenly, a moan came from an unspecified spot in the room. Everybody turned around. On a big armchair covered with a black, withered fabric that made it look like a monstrous garbage bag, was lying a human bundle, or better a sack of bones once assembled in a human female form. A pair of jeans and a hoodie as big as a tent were sadly hanging loose on her body. Helen barely had time to register this information, when the skinnier guy at the table addressed the dark, gloomy woman, that, until then, had been staying quiet.

"Hey, lady!" he called to her in a half-tired, half-annoyed tone, "this is the third time you've come, this week. And you never bring us shit!"

Helen looked at a dark, gloomy woman and her husband, confused. The tour participants were snooping around, and nobody seemed to have paid any attention to that inference, not even Warren, who was busy staring at the photographer, who, squatted on his heels in a dusty corner of the room, was aiming the lenses of his camera upwards, trying to catch the table from that perspective. Was it possible the woman was so attracted to this kind of tour, that she would take part in them with such frequency? Helen turned to her husband to share her puzzlement, when the sack of bones raised up from her nest and dragged herself towards them, with the strenuous motions of someone who had just woken up. She was muttering something incomprehensible.

It was then, staring at the blank eyes of that skeleton, that Helen realised that the gaunt features of that devastated face were identical to those of the dark, gloomy woman. The latter was staring at the withered, approaching figure as if she was looking at herself rising from the grave, her eyes were red but steely and hostile, hardened by the pain, and from the emaciated girl she received just an empty look of acknowledgment and a constant utterance, "sparechangesparechangesparechange", a slurry and monotonous litany, which from all the tossing and turning in her mouth it started to not make any sense, like food that's been chewed for too long loses its taste.

Guido got in the way, pushing himself through the small crowd. He had now lost all restraint and was pervaded by an orgiastic enthusiasm.

"A photo! A photo with the walking dead!" he screamed, grabbing a random protruding bone and pulling the girl close.

Unexpectedly, the dark, gloomy woman's husband flung himself at Guido with a beastly growl, grabbing him by the collar. Al immediately rushed forward to hold him, in a gesture perhaps dictated by habit, the same habit that led him to put his hands on Guido as soon as he, in the confusion of the moment, elbowed him in the face. There was a great swirling of elbows and knees. Janine yelling, tried to separate them, but the difference in body structure was so abyssal, the two men practically swallowed her. She disappeared somewhere around Al's belly. Warren and the reporter exchanged glances, feeling obliged to intervene. They tried to drag Al away by grabbing him, one took his right arm, the other the left one, ducking punches and kicks at the same time. The sack of bones had slipped from Guido's grasp and had slid to the floor in a liturgy of protests interspersed with requests for money. The guys sitting at the table stood up, dragging their chairs and pushing the table to the side, in a feeble choir of protests. Ashtrays spilled and bottles rolled. The Molossian, sensing the turmoil, began to bark, and the action was immediately mirrored by the Countess's little piranha-dog, whose eyes seemed on the verge of popping out of their sockets. Trapped in a corner, Helen observed the scene, petrified, her purse clutched tightly to her chest, like a shield. The dark, gloomy woman was frozen in place in the centre of the room, and it seemed that she wasn't even aware of the hell that was breaking out around her. Her eyes were fixed on the sack of bones, who was creepy crawling her way towards Guido's phone, that had fallen during the fight and was now lying on the floor.

From the other room, Alex rushed in with the cattle prod.

"What's going on here?"

He was about to take aim, when he realised he couldn't taser his own clients.

"Help us!" Warren yelled to him, dodging a jab aimed at the bridge of his nose.

Alex and the blond guy dove into that rough-and-tumble brawl, and the four of them pulled Al back, who pulled the gloomy man back, who pulled Guido back, whom felt dragged from all sides, and even before the cop intervened, had already put his hands up in surrender. Janine was spat out like a pinball, disheveled and half-beaten. Al appeared almost possessed, and he was foaming at the mouth like the Molossian held back by his owner on the other side of the room. Guido resurfaced outraged, and even dirtier than before, which gave his character at least an inch of authenticity, but Warren didn't feel like telling him so. Janine was livid.

"Gentlemen, this situation is most unfortunate!" Alex gasped, astounded. He was aware of the fact that he was scolding men twice his age, and it sounded awkward, embarrassing and dramatically poor in credibility. Amongst all the incidents that had occurred in this job, it was the first time something like this had happened to him. "Whatever the reason for the dispute, I have to ask you to refrain from such saloon scenes, or I'll be forced to cancel your participation. This is a rough environment, and this kind of behavior agitates and excites the subjects in the wrong way. Gentlemen, I must say I am shocked. Shocked."

The Countess uttered a noise of haughty disapproval, as to show that she had nothing to do with that rabble. The girl belonging to the little family was on the verge of tears. The guys at the table sat down again to better enjoy the show, and they were laughing nastily. The younger one with the glasses repeatedly tapped a finger to his forehead.

"Oh, your fat cats, are they nuts, or what?"

"Put them on a leash, meow, meow!" the other one echoed, with a crooked smile.

The sack of bones had climbed onto a chair and sat there, one palm over her temples as if she was suffering from a massive headache, murmuring a string of "idiots, I stole nothing, change."

"And now, I would ask you to resume the tour without any further disruptions," Alex concluded, with the same embarrassed severity, before turning his back to the group and moving forward towards the hallway, in what in his mind was a leadership trait.

The husband of the dark, gloomy woman was twisted and misty-eyed. He grabbed his wife by the arm and tried to drag her away by force. He wasn't able to move her an inch. It looked as if she was anchored to the ground, as if she had taken root in that sticky, stinking floor. Exhausted, the man murmured something in her ear, and very slowly he was able to unscrew her from her position. The woman let herself be pulled away as if she had no willpower to control her own actions, and she was dragged away, pushed by the group retreating to the hallway. The sack of bones was totally indifferent to what was taking place in front of her. She was confusedly rolling a smoke with greasy hands, babbling about one dude named 'Planer', who had promised to come at a certain time.

It was just then that Helen realised that her hands ached. She lowered her gaze to the purse: she was clutching it so hard that her knuckles had become white. Suddenly, the contents of that purse, the purse itself she had chosen with such care, seemed meaningless to her.

Guido was removing from his hair microscopic particles of filth that weren't included in his costume, and from which he probably didn't want to be infected. He couldn't stop mumbling dazed and offended exclamations to himself.

"I can't believe it," he proclaimed, brushing his trousers and dirtying them even more with his filthy hands. "An assault of this kind...I'm taking you to court, do you understand? To court!" he screamed. His voice echoed in the empty hallway.

"Come on, Guido, let's go!" Warren beckoned to him, taking him by the arm.

They had been left alone in the room, with three junkies and a Pitbull that was still sniffing the tense atmosphere and growling in a threatening way. While they were about to leave, Guido stumbled in his worn-out shoes, and had to lean on Warren's arm.

"Yo, watch out!" one of the two junkies said to their backs, a shade of half-mocked concern in his voice.

Nobody turned around to reply.

Helen stiffened, fully aware that her calves must have looked a delectable treat, seen from behind and wrapped in transparent hose. She hurried, trying not to show it, but the noise of her heels exposed to the onlookers all of her weakness and cowardice.

"Freaks," she heard the same voice commenting, as they left the room.

# SEWAGE

"Da-aaad!" Chrissy's annoyed voice chanted from the hallway.

It mattered little that *he* wasn't her real dad, it was for some time now that her mother had let him move in. Bob rose from the couch at the third call. On screen, a reporter in the bleachers was interviewing a sports fan who gesticulated wildly, raptured in his own reasoning, and was speaking in a loud voice to be heard among the excited buzzing and throbbing of the stadium, absentmindedly hitting with his elbows a man wearing a hat and a turquoise scarf, who sat next to him and stared intently at something in front of him. The national anthem moment was due to start any minute, now. The trilling voice called again. Bob couldn't resist her syrupy inflection, but it better be important to disturb him while he was watching the game.

Chrissy, all of sixteen years old, was leaning on the bathroom door frame with her hands on her narrow hips, all dressed up. She was chewing gum with a disgusted look.

"That stupid sink ate one of my earrings, again! I can see it from here. It's stuck in the drain."

Bob snorted. He pulled up the stretched out elastic waistband of his sweatpants over his jutting belly, and bent over the sink, grunting. The empty drain hole stared at him, swallowing his gaze like a dark, endless pit.

"I wouldn't place my face so close to the hole, if I were you," he heard Alice chirping from somewhere behind his back. "A monster lives in there. A monster with very long nails. The other day I looked inside, and I saw his eye. He's not very friendly."

Chrissy sneered, shifting from one leg to the other. Bob tensed up, feeling a familiar anger rising inside him. Alice knew that he couldn't stand this kind of foolishness. More than once, he had to hit her, because she was inclined to losing herself in inane fantasies. She should have followed her older sister's example. Chrissy was so mature, sweet and level-headed: a real sugar plum. Bob was a very practical man. Anything that went beyond the basic concept of home, work and television was already too extravagant for his taste. He barely turned his head to look at the kid. Alice stood still in the doorway, holding her disheveled doll in her arms.

"Shut. Your Mouth." he snarled, every word a threat. "How many times I've warned you our family doesn't need to put up with your bullshit!"

He went back to his task, and he pressed his eye to look deep down the drain, as if he was trying to get inside the siphon. Yeah, he could see it. There it was that goddamn earring...

At that moment he was struck by an excruciating pain that blinded him. Bob fell backwards, slamming against the sanitary fittings, his hands, quickly filling with blood, pressed to his face.

His dreadful screams echoed around the room, while Chrissy stared incredulously at the sink, and saw a protruding claw slowly retreating down the drain. An eyeball dripping blood impaled on its sharp tip.

"I told him not to put his face too close to the hole," Alice remarked with a mischievous little grimace, brushing the hair of the doll with her pudgy fingers.

# FACTS, NOT WORDS

The light of the dying sun hit the walls of the house, painting the urban landscape with scenic mountain valley postcard shades.

Grace came out of the building, putting her sunglasses on, searching her jacket pockets to make sure she had the keys. Because of the meeting with those two assholes, she had been forced to leave the studio early, and she still had to speak with the gallerist about the last details for the exhibit. This was absolutely the last thing she needed.

She climbed down the steps and waved to the building's caretaker. The woman leaned out of the entrance.

"Say hi to your Ian!"

"Will do!" Grace replied, with a broad smile. That was typical Ian, everywhere he went, he seemed to make an impression. Everybody liked him.

The elementary school's educational collaborator also always had a kind word about him, too. Grace remembered when she attended school they were called 'janitors', but the word had been considered offensive, and it had been replaced by educational collaborator. The apron they were wearing, however, was the same as Grace remembered. The woman was large and jolly and knew them well by then. Every time Grace went to pick up Robin, they performed the same routine. The lady leaned out of her lodge in the hall, and asked:

"Can I see your ID?"

Grace put on an exasperated smile. The woman winked at her, crossing her arms on her generous chest.

"Yeah, I know, there's no need. I am well aware of who you are. But you understand, it's a formality."

So, Grace handed her the document, and the woman scanned it into the computer. They both agreed on the whole procedure was ridiculous. Sometimes, the computer crashed, using such a rigorous method was simply painful. It remained memorable the time a mother came to pick up her daughter, but the system didn't recognise her document. The educational collaborator on duty had been inflexible. The girl had waited for hours, crying and screeching, until her other parent came to collect her with a valid ID.

When the electronic sound announced the hall pass was authorised, Robin passed through the turnstile, the lady waved goodbye from her lodge, and said as always:

"Say hi to your Ian!"

"Your Ian" wasn't pronounced just as a courtesy with a slight powdery, archaic taste, but was a full-fledged definition of status. Grace and Ian weren't married, and there still didn't exist a word to describe their relationship. The word 'partner' had fallen into disuse ages ago. Too political, they said. It risked creating confusion, grey areas, and discontent, which is not what was expected by a civil society. "Your Ian" had been invented precisely by the big educational collaborator, after she had not seen him for a while. She had greeted Grace enthusiastically, resting her hands on her hips: "And how's your Ian?"

Since then, it had remained "your Ian" substituting "consort" or "companion", just like Grace became "your Grace", which somehow made that whole mayhem even funnier. They started to use it every time the subject came up. Ian found it to be romantic; Grace found that it covered their asses at the parent-teacher meetings. They fought for it to be validated on a legal level. The lines, and the amount of paperwork to make the name legal on official documents had been endless, gigantic, and complicated. The first accusation on the other side was why they didn't want to get married.

Personal reasons were the vague motivation given in response, most of the times the functionaries shrugged, but declared it wasn't a situation to be tolerated. That's why they started to accept it as a preventive measure, because the absence of a term to describe their sentimental status was unacceptable. Whenever a private citizen was the one requesting to change words in the vocabulary, it seemed to take triple of time.

Sighing, Grace looked around her. A man wearing a hat and a turquoise scarf was waiting his turn at an ice cream kiosk on the corner of the street. Grace got stuck looking at the colour of his scarf, before the direction of her gaze turned right, lured by the shining whiteness of a refined window shop displaying fresh seasonal flowers. She thought that buying roses to put in the centrepiece would have brighten the room, and maybe create a peaceful atmosphere that would cool off the two harpies. When it came to their children, some parents could reach levels of hysteria which bordered on cruelty.

She pushed open the glass door, which emitted a jingling sound, and addressed with a gracious smile the woman behind the counter, who waited motionless, standing straight in the empty shop with the severe look of a Flemish painting.

"Good morning. I would like a bouquet of red roses, please."

The woman stared at her as if she had been asked to stab herself in the chest with a pair of her shears.

"Excuse me?"

"Roses. Red. Please." Grace repeated, bewildered by that scandalised reaction.

"Don't you know?" the woman retorted, bitterly spinning around every syllable in her mouth. "Congress has decided that 'rose' is a sexist word to indicate this kind of flower. It implies that it's destined just for individuals of a specific sex for whom the colour is addressed and conceived."

"What? But that's ridiculous!" Grace cut in.

The woman ignored her.

"So, unanimously, the change of nomenclature has been made. The term rose has fallen into disuse. Now, the correct word is 'less red'."

Grace blinked, stunned.

"But it's a rose."

The woman held her gaze, defiantly.

"No. It's a less red."

Grace sighed.

"All right," she said, "but don't you think this could produce a terrible linguistic chaos? What would happen if, let's say, I'd ask you for a blue less red?"

The scandalised expression on that lemon face was sufficient to let Grace understand she must have used another forbidden word, and, breathing deeply, she immediately backed off.

"All right. What will happen if I'd ask you for an azure less red?"

"Blue and all its gradations have been suppressed," the lemon face mechanically replied, through gritted teeth. "No more light blue, azure or cerulean. Now we say: 'less black'."

"Blue is a primary colour," Grace protested "So I imagine that this beautiful thought does not only concern botany, but the word per se. When I buy tempera paints, I'll have to ask for an 'ultramarine less black'?"

"Do you really believe it was better, before?" the lemon face asked her. "That asking for a rose-coloured rose was clearer, more decent, and linguistically appropriate?"

"It was, if you were well aware of what you were talking about. This way, we'll end up being so careful about embellishments, we'll forget the essence of things," Grace rebutted.

The woman had the expression of a colonist of Her Majesty in front of a wild half-naked native.

"You don't seem to be really up-to-date on the national vocabulary. Can I ask you what business you are in?" she asked, oozing civility out of every pore.

"I'm an artist," Grace curtly replied. "I'm not updated because I am holed up all day in my studio, painting, and I assure you that, on canvas, a rose stays a rose. Doesn't matter how you want to call it."

An awkward silence fell.

Grace was breathing like a scuba diver. It was crystal clear the woman deemed her a barbaric reactionary, but business rules, and an education built on broad views prevented her from kicking that despicable creature out of her shop.

"All right," she was forced to yield, eventually. "Give me a bouquet of red less reds, please?"

Without a word, the lemon face prepared the flowers, spreading an even larger yellow aura of bitterness. Grace paid and left without saying goodbye.

"They have to be kidding me!" she announced, as soon as she got home, placing her keys on the small table in the entrance.

"Hm?" uttered Ian, or better, uttered Ian's butt, protruding from the door frame. He was bent over the oven. The room smelled deliciously of sugary flour and yeast. "Not that I have false modesty, but this time I really outdid myself!" he proclaimed, rubbing his hands on the apron he was wearing. "We'll take the two caimans by the throat. What's with the flowers?"

"I bought them for the two barracudas," Grace tiredly replied, "to decorate the living room for their delicate eyes, so maybe they'll calm down. I still can't believe it."

Ian leaned on the doorjamb, and looked her in the eyes, sensing her irritation.

"Are you still mad because I didn't feel like taking the tablet away from Robin? Listen, in my opinion he didn't do anything that horrible to deserve being punished." He held Grace's twisted look without batting an eye. "It's just a comic book."

"Ian, we can't keep on being so indulgent. Things are different, now. You want to know what happened at the flower shop?"

She briefly summarised her visit to the place.

"I heard something similar on the news. The vocabulary being updated." Ian looked less surprised than he should have been.

"Do you see?" Grace protested, while opening drawers in pursuit of a vase. "Before comic books, now this?"

Ian straightened up from the position he had taken to check the pie.

"Remember what Robin told us, about the school motto?" he said.

"Speak clean, or do not speak at all?" Grace recited, with a shiver. "We're living in an age of collective hysteria, I'm telling you. They're all hunting for non-existing ghosts."

Ian shrugged.

"They closed the film libraries," Grace insisted. "For, quote-unquote, 'revision'. What's behind all this? Soon enough, they'll burn all the remaining books. There are some old paper editions you can't find anymore. All the new digital ones are edited, as you should well know. Don't you think we're past those measure, now?"

"Well, at least now my collections will be worth tons of money, before they were just useless junk," Ian joked, turning off the oven.

"Laugh now - just wait until they press charges against you. That saleswoman looked like she wanted to call the police. And I remind you we found ourselves in this situation, in this exact moment, to put a patch on a ridiculous situation to avoid from spreading."

"You are worrying too much."

"Don't you realise that bitch wanted to set up a parent-teachers committee conference?" Grace protested, arranging the flowers in the vase. She felt belittled in her anger. "All hell was about to break loose. I don't even know how I eventually managed to solve the issue in private, without involving the institutions."

"Because you're a great moderator," Ian replied, untying his apron.

"Look, I agree with you. There's a tendency towards overprotection and thus a word classification so strict and excessive as to be ridiculous, but the intentions behind it are good. It all leads to the will to create a decent, more tolerant world. They are measures taken in good faith."

"When you start fearing words it's time to worry," Grace grumbled, running a hand through her hair.

"You're speaking as a visual artist," Ian said, giving her a peck on the cheek. "You go straight to the facts. Let them bask in their baths of polished expressions. We'll eat them in a bite, like my fabulous pie."

The doorbell rang. Ian squeezed her shoulders in an embrace.

"Give me your best smile."

Grace contorted her face in a lunatic grimace. Ian laughed. Fixing her underpants that had gotten stuck between her butt cheeks, Grace went to open the door.

"It's so good to see you!" she tweeted, flashing a toothpaste-advertisement smile. "Please, come in, don't stand outside!"

Peter and Karin Inkstetten were standing tall and stiff in the doorway, seeping money and country estates out of every hole.

He was a mountain of a man, with a pair of azure, nervous eyes shining in his bald head, making his face look like a skull. His body matched in size the power of his career position, and he was clearly accustomed to using both to intimidate, and with some success. She was a gangly, lanky woman, as if a pair of hands had held her by the extremities and stretched her towards opposite ends. In her eyes, shone the same energetic sparkle as her husband, the look of those people who had never had to apologise for anything in their lives. She was the founder as well the most active participant of the Child Defence

School Committee, also being the President and Administrator of all the parent-teachers meeting in the classes attended by their children. Grace couldn't particularly stand her, first of all because she knew Karin openly disapproved of her sentimental status; then, because on account of her, every quarrel among classmates had to be dutifully reported and investigated thoroughly (under the President's jurisdiction, of course) by an assembly of mothers, whom had to verify case by case the gravity of the situation, and debate the most appropriate way to deal with it. Needless to say, fights in an elementary class occurred on a daily basis, and the whole issue consumed a monstrous amount of time. To exasperate things more, if you did not attend those meetings more than twice, you were subjected to an actual intervention, where the President and two members of the committee came knocking at your door, to understand if the reasons of the absence were sufficiently excusable, and to make sure parents hadn't brought a child into the world, only to lead him astray.

The couple made their way through the entrance.

"Come in, sit down, take off your coats," Grace offered, laden with courtesy.

"Pretty chilly, huh?" Ian stated, shaking Peter's hand. "Let's light a fire, shall we?"

"It's lovely here," Karin commented, with the voice of someone who didn't believe it.

"Is Kristian at the after-school activity?" Grace trilled, taking the overcoat Karin was handing her.

"Yeah, he's at swimming practice."

"Robin chose basketball, instead," Grace informed them, just to make conversation. "Even if sometimes it is so difficult getting him ready to go.

If it were up to him, he'd spend all his time locked in his room playing with his tablet!"

"I hope you installed parental control," Karin retorted, with a courtesy as cold and unpleasant as an ice block on a dog turd.

Grace was caught by surprise as she turned towards the coat rack. She felt her back stiffen.

"Sure, I did," she replied, with a voice like broken glass. She turned her back on Karin to hang up Peter's coat, and she heard Karin justifying herself.

"Well, you know how it is...you may never know."

"Something to drink?" offered Ian, who had missed the whole scene. "A little good cheer?"

The Inkstettens asked for two glasses of mineral water with lemon.

They all sat down on the sofa in front of the fireplace, near the coffee table where Grace had arranged the flowers. Ian came from the kitchen, bringing four glasses and four slices of pie nobody felt like eating. In the general silence, Mr. Inkstetten asked politely for a toothpick. The atmosphere was filled with an oppressive, tense courtesy.

The guests nibbled at the pie out of politeness and duly lavishing ritual compliments.

"You need to give me the recipe," Karin asked Grace, graciously cleaning the corners of her mouth with the napkin.

"Then you'll have to ask me," Ian chimed in, smiling. "I was the one who made the pie."

"Oh!" Karin exclaimed, pleasantly surprised. Peter coughed.

"Well!" Grace rumbled, seizing the right moment to address the elephant in the room. "Shall we get straight to the point?"

Karin uttered the noise of someone who suddenly remembers a regrettable situation.

"I must confess," she started with gravity, "initially, when we found the comic, we unfairly blamed our son. We thought he stole it from somewhere, some place where certain boys hide indecent stuff...but when he told us it was Robin who gave it to him, and that he had even brought it from home...frankly, we were shocked. That's why we wanted to see you." She paused to look Grace in the eyes. "We asked ourselves: 'what's going on?'"

"We are here to clear any doubt," Grace replied, spreading her arms, and thinking, *what you're not saying is that you came by to check on 'what's going on' in this house. Bitch.*

"Good!" Peter announced, and he addressed the other man in a confidential tone. "I calmed her down and convinced her to accept this meeting. If it were for her, she'd already have reported you guys to the authorities!"

He winked at Ian as if to say: "women, so apprehensive and always overreacting!" Karin chuckled.

"Yes, I have to admit I have the sin of impulsiveness. It's just that I find it unacceptable that this kind of material gets spread among our children, especially in an educational context such as school. Corruption on malleable minds is a practice I just can't bear. Luckily..." and there she smiled sweetly at her husband "Peter explained to me that everybody deserves a chance to account for themselves."

Ian put a hand on Grace's knee, sensing that she was already starting to vibrate like a metronome.

Karin opened her purse and took out a yellowed comic book holding it by the edge, as if until that moment it had been immersed in the toilet bowl. She put it on the coffee table where it lay, dead, among flowers and dessert plates.

It was an old print of a once famous children's comic book that came out weekly, dated back forty years before. On the cover, there was a dog, the protagonist of the adventures, with a musket behind his back. Over the picture stood out big yellow writing that read: 'DINKY THE DOG'.

"As soon as I discovered it, I had the impulse to destroy it," Karin commented, looking at the comic book with resentment, as if it had offended her. "But then, I didn't do it."

"And rightly so," Grace highlighted with tenderness. "It would have been like destroying someone else's property, and this is not a good thing, right?"

"*None* should own such things," Karin replied without smiling back. "And most of all give it to his own son, given *what* is drawn on it."

"And what is drawn on it?" Grace patiently spoonfed her.

"Can't you see for yourself?" Karin looked at her as if she was stupid. "Guns!" she spat out, with the tone of one who has been exorcised, spitting out the devil. "Right there, in front of your eyes, there's a dog with a rifle."

"Sure, because he hunts hares," Grace butted in, "which seems to me a perfectly normal activity for a dog."

Karin put on the face of someone who had just heard a direct insult to his mother.

"If it's normal to you, a comic book aimed at children that shows this kind of violence fully displayed…"

"Well, you can't see the *corpse* of the hare, right?" Grace questioned.

Karin icily glared at her.

"Are you pretending you don't understand? It's the symbol. The rifle is a symbol of hate, and instigates unacceptable behavior, to shoot another living creature. A child may think to copy the character in class with his peers, as a joke, with any weapons at his disposal. Plastic scissors, blocks. Can you imagine what would happen if they started to throw rulers into each other's eyes? I don't want my son to be exposed to those kinds of risks, and it should be an essential parental duty to monitor literature given to minors."

"We are aware of it," Ian said, conciliatory. "Perfectly. Thing is… you see, Robin…our son, he found this comic book while he was digging in the basement. He was playing and found it, among the myriad of old magazines, and other thingamabob it was buried under. The comic book wasn't in the house."

"Well, you should have locked it away, then," Peter chimed in, in his dulcet tones. "So that he couldn't have got to it, couldn't reach it. If we apply the principle you just stated to everything, even the liquor cabinet, it's not dangerous until your son puts his hands on the vodka."

"I wonder why a civil person would keep such an item," Karin ganged up.

"Because it's history? It's memories?" Grace rebutted pretty straightforwardly.

"Some memories would be better consigned to oblivion," Peter said with quiet coldness. "We know full well, for example, that some historical periods weren't exactly happy times."

"When it comes to protecting the souls of those easily impressed," Karin sentenced "I believe history should be rewritten."

Grace failed to hide the spasm of horror that crossed her face.

"Do you have a gun in your house?" she vehemently asked, ignoring Ian's hand, that was trying to admonish her.

"Sure," Karin said, surprised. "What does that have to do with anything?"

"And why do you have one? It's been supplied as a state safeguard measure, right?"

"Absolutely," Peter agreed.

"We live in a country where a gun is given to every family, and people attend military preparation courses, and you're putting up a fight for a rifle drawn on a dog's back?" Grace burst out, slamming her glass on the coffee table.

The Inkstettens exchanged a puzzled look.

"Sorry, but I don't follow your thinking," Peter said with a weak grin. "It's almost as if you are in favor of stealing."

"What would we do, otherwise, in the matter of personal defence?" his wife supported him.

"The point is," Mr. Inkstetten resumed, chewing on his toothpick, "the child has been exposed to inappropriate images while he should have been under the supervision of an adult. We're not talking about a governmental provision addressed to adult, sentient users."

Grace didn't like the tone of that inference, at all.

She knew that Karin had launched a campaign named 'Presence Guardian', calling for the government to establish a law forcing one of the parents to stay home with their child, to guarantee the minor sufficient care and attention, and not to leave him 'unattended' for too long. Mrs. Inkstetten claimed that such a measure ensured an amount of affection and presence that prevented bullying and exclusion amongst children. Ian had branded the entire issue as bullshit, but Grace believed it was dangerous, instead. A lot of parents had signed the petition, which raised the level of that initiative higher than just the delusion of a poor lunatic.

"It makes you wonder how it is possible, that a child could have come into contact with such pictures, if maybe, with two working parents, he wasn't left alone for too long," the lunatic in question was indeed arguing.

"It's a DRAWING," Grace exploded, feeling as frustrated as a trapped mouse.

"It's a *model*" Karin retorted, "like, on page twenty. There's a character smoking."

"Oh, yeah. It's Kitty the Cat, Dinky's sidekick, and partner in crime," Ian chimed in, with a nostalgic undertone that, in that context, sounded absolutely incongruous. "She's always carrying her inseparable pipe."

"Honestly, you think it's a picture to introduce to such an easily influenced audience as the pre-teen one?" Karin reproachfully weighed in. "We wouldn't want them, at such a young age, to develop the vice of smoking because they read this kind of rubbish."

Grace was totally taken aback.

"They are children, they're not dumb!"

"This may not be the adjective we are looking for, here," Peter coughed.

"The model is the first point," Karin repeated, with the strength of a religious fanatic repeating a prayer. "Do you smoke, in this house?"

"No," belligerently replied Grace.

The expression on the face of Mrs. Inkstetten was of pure disappointment.

"It is scientifically proven that children learn from what they see, through a process of repetition and reiteration," Peter explained, in a professional tone. "Imagine what would happen if such material started to appear in the children's section of the bookstores."

"Some great classics like 'The Adventures of Sherlock Holmes', in the version reserved for the youngest, have already been modified in regard to the display of bad habits," his wife commented, sounding satisfied.

"The great detective doesn't smoke his pipe anymore, but he's obsessed with liquorice," Mr. Inkstetten concluded, pleased as if it was all thanks to him.

"And do you really think this is a useful precautionary measure?" asked Grace.

Mr. Inkstetten shot her a sincerely surprised look.

"Well, it's obvious. After all, we simply followed the line of our predecessor, who had expurgated the children's copies of other unedifying elements, such as substance abuse."

Karin cleared her throat, as if just mentioning the words 'substance abuse' could turn the living room into the front desk of an addiction treatment centre.

"Look, what do you want us to do?" Ian yielded. He was starting to lose his patience. "Do you want us to get rid of those comic books?"

"Ian, I don't see why we should do that," angrily protested Grace. "That material is a valuable collection, and I don't mean just in monetary terms. It's your memories."

"The precautionary action to take is yet to be decided," Mr. Inkstetten piped up promptly, as if Grace didn't talk at all.

"Precautionary action?" echoed Ian.

"Towards Robin," the other one replied as if stating the obvious.

"Excuse me, but, for now, I think I can reserve the right to decide what's the most suitable punishment for my son," Ian icily responded. "I'm still his father, and I am the person responsible for these tasks."

"I am not so sure about that," Mr. Inkstetten retorted. "Unfortunately, this situation doesn't involve just you. The decision on what should be done, will be left up to the majority of the assembly."

"The decision on 'what should be done' to my son?" Ian's voice was sepulchral. "What is that supposed to mean?"

"In regard to his removal from school or not," Peter Inkstetten calmly announced. "You see, we as parents can't afford other children to be exposed to the risk your son put Kristian through. Exposure to this kind of violent, offensive language makes him a danger to himself, and his schoolmates. After all, even one rotten apple in the barrel..."

"Did you just call my son a rotten apple?" Grace snapped.

"All fruit can rot, if it's not given the right attention," Karin chimed in, voice all syrupy.

"What are you trying to imply?" Grace asked, tuning her voice to a hysterical key, against her own will. "That we are not able to take care of our son?"

Ian placed a hand on her arm.

"I didn't say that," Karin hurriedly replied, in a vague tone. "It's just that, given the ease with which the child was able to get this kind of violent material, the environment he lives in should not be considered perfectly secure..."

"You know what?" Grace curtly yielded. "You win. You want that comic book to disappear forever? Easily done. Tonight, we'll go down to the basement, and we'll get rid of all the boxes."

"I do not think this is the point anymore," Karin sweetly said, staring into Grace's eyes. "The real question here, my dear, is: how far can art go? I believe that you, as a painter, have already given yourself an answer. And I'm afraid it's not the answer the community is looking for."

Grace felt the blood chilling in her veins.

"What are you trying to say?"

"I'm just saying that, when a situation is considered to be risky, the State has adequate measures to deal with it," Karin defensively coughed. "There's a long list of families suitable for the protection of the child, and if the child's parents have his safety seriously at heart, they could..."

A horrific feeling washed over Grace; a dreadful suspicion had gripped her since the beginning of the conversation, and was now being confirmed.

She jerked up, making the glasses clink.

"You're not taking away my son!"

"Now, now, take it easy," Peter chanted, in the bored voice of someone trying to contain a scene.

"I must ask you to leave," Grace said, struggling to keep her voice steady.

She marched with determination towards the coat rack, hearing a chorus of polite protests exploding behind her back. It hurt her to hear Ian's voice joining that chorus, calling after her with the patient tone one uses with an unreasonable child.

She grabbed coat and overcoat, almost tearing them off the coat rack, not caring if she balled them up with her rushed gestures.

"Grace," she heard Ian calling behind her. He had followed her into the entrance. "I am sure it's not what they mean - Grace! Let's not complicate things!"

Without looking at him, she brushed past, pushing him aside as if he were an obstacle. Ian followed after her, sighing.

From the couch, Karin had stood up, and was muttering something in a hushed voice. Her husband was still settled comfortably on the couch, as if the hostess had not invited him to pack it up.

Grace threw the coats on the back of the sofa, rudely.

"Nice manners," Peter protested.

"Out." Grace retorted, curtly.

"Listen..." started Karin, in a reasonable, tranquil tone, putting her hand on Grace's back.

Grace angrily wriggled away from her grip as if she had been burnt.

"Don't touch me!"

Thereby, her arm hit Karen's, who pulled back horrified, as if she had received the crack of a whip. Mr. Inkstetten immediately stood up from his throne, and interposed himself between the two women, in defence of his lady, as if Grace had assaulted her.

"Keep your hands to yourself, we don't want things to escalate," he bantered courteously undertoned with menace.

In a flash, a savage light flickered in his eyes, something that wasn't there until that moment. Ian didn't like the vehemence of that gesture, and got in between as well, shielding Grace.

"It doesn't feel right to revert to violence, don't you think?" Peter threatened grinning, with the low growl of a stray dog challenged for the possession of the last bone. An almost sadistic sneer was now painted on his lips.

He towered over Ian by at least four inches, but he refused to be intimidated, and didn't bat an eyelash.

"Grace already asked you to leave. It seems clear to me you're not welcome, here," he replied, unperturbed. He was raising the stakes.

"Well, there are many different ways to ask for something, decent people treat the others with courtesy," Peter barked in a sinister tone, closing the distance between them.

Grace perceived in the air that kind of nervous energy that forewarns a duel, so palpable you could slice it. She addressed Karin, who was peeking, afraid, from behind her strong husband's back.

"That's enough. Get out of our house, please," she ordered, but to her ears it sounded horrifyingly like a prayer.

"See? She said 'please', so pick up your things and go away," Ian stoically added, without taking a step back.

Peter kept on getting closer, now drunk with testosterone, lost to the call of male conflict. Ian sounded like a broken record, and kept on repeating the same sentence, 'she said please, so go away', as if he were stuck. Peter overlapped that litany with phrases growled in such a low tone as to result unintelligible, sounding dangerously similar to 'politeness is what you need in life' and 'with calm and kindness, you can obtain everything'.

It wasn't clear what spring had snapped in his brain, when Ian, without further notice, stopped his liturgy and finally pushed the man away, breaking the spell of that absurd balance.

Peter grabbed the poker from the fireplace, and threw it with all his might at Ian, who collapsed to the ground. Grace screamed. Karin was crying. Ian's body had fallen like a bowling pin, and was now laying on the ground, in an unnatural position. Thick, dark blood slowly poured onto the floor, rapidly soaking into the rug. Ian's eyes were motionless, and the room smelled like iron and shit. Grace was terrified, she couldn't move a muscle. She was frozen, hands clutched to her mouth, and she was just able to think that, for some ridiculous reason, living blood seemed less real than the bright one in her paintings, and the hues of its colour were more rose-coloured, much, much more rose-coloured.

# THE SEED

Legs spread open on the ob-gyn stretcher; Paula was overcome with emotion.

The doctor's probe was affectionately rubbing the smooth depression of her barely outlined belly, round like the surface of a planet, as the greyish, gibbous stain reproduced on screen, emerging from the blackness of the amniotic liquid, resembled the surface of the moon in the stellar darkness of outer space.

It still seemed incredible to her that the blurred shape was the evident proof of the existence of life. The child had been strongly desired, desperately awaited, never arrived. She hadn't thought that she would ever have experienced that unexpected joy. She and Ned had worked so hard. She let her glance turn from the screen to her husband, who held her hand tightly, glowing. The doctor looked at the couple with a kind smile. She let them enjoy their happiness for a few more minutes, then, in the warm, reprimanding tone of a good but severe teacher, she reminded her patient that to pass a serene pregnancy she must absolutely not subject her body to any kind of stress and scrupulously follow the prescribed diet. Paula said yes to everything, moved. She was aware she was a little over the hill for a first pregnancy, but she would have managed it in the best possible way. She would have granted the baby all it needed to make it a happy creature. She was sure she could have raised it with the same energy with which she had desired it, even if she wasn't in her twenties anymore, and not even in her thirties. What had happened, could have been defined as a miracle. For years they had hoped, despaired, strived and suffered. They had tried everything. Doctor appointments, great luminaries. Without telling her husband, who was more the rational, analytical type, Paula had even consulted a witch doctor. It was all for nothing. Medical records showed that both she and Ned were indeed able to have children. It was just that her uterus was less welcoming than others, and Ned's sperm cells were a bit lazy. It seemed there was absolutely nothing wrong them. And yet, somehow, life wouldn't take root. It had been suggested that Ned's sperm just needed to be stimulated; that Paula's uterus was just a little bit too slippery, her eggs too shy. They both had taken the appropriate measures in order to meet their needs, pointlessly.

Artificial insemination had frightened Ned due to costs and obstacles, and Paula couldn't have tolerated the seed of the person she loved had to be planted in a ground more fertile than hers. She felt inhospitable, barren, desert-like. Blame and responsibility ping-ponged. Quarrels, crying and sleepless nights. Sure, there had been good times, carefree interludes in which they told themselves they were happy with each other. But those moments were permeated by that melancholic, unpleasant sensation of incompleteness. More than once they had questioned their relationship, but they loved each other, and they had endured everything. The ordeal had lasted fifteen years. Then, at last, the miracle. They couldn't have found any other definition to describe it, because nothing had worked, surely not the philosophy of relax and don't think it, it will happen. It did happen, out of the blue. When she had seen the positive sign on the pregnancy test, a knot in Paula's chest that had been suffocating her, loosened, and she finally felt she could breathe again.

"Do you want to know the sex of the baby?" the kind doctor asked.

"Is it already possible?"

It was possible.

"Congratulations. It's a girl," the woman announced, caressing Paula's belly with her probe.

The couple looked at each other, moved. They have often had talked about that, during their daytime fantasies. Paula had always dreamed of having a baby girl. She would have blonde hair, like her mom, and her name would have been Melanie.

Pregnancy for Paula was an unexpectedly serene period. Several friends had warned her of morning sickness, swollen feet, weight gain, high blood pressure, mood changes, sudden cravings, hemorrhoids and pregnancy acne. Her gynecologist had already prescribed a diet. None of these disastrous symptoms fell on Paula. Her body seemed suitable to host a life with the exact same stubbornness with which it had pushed it away a few months earlier. She was glowing. She felt beautiful, she was beautiful. Her figure molded evenly, almost elegantly, without the typical deformations that go with pregnancy. She harmoniously made space for the new tenant. She seemed spared all the troubles and the downside of pregnancy, as if carrying a child were for her the ideal condition of existence.

It was almost at the end of the third quarter that in her head started swirling the idea that she didn't want that condition to end. She realised she had been regulating her needs on those of the baby, with whom she felt to have sealed an osmotic bond. She wasn't sure she wanted to give it up already. Thinking about being divided at the end of the ninth month, the irreparable split from the intimacy of her womb, was for her cause of immeasurable pain. Not to mention when, further in time, when the child would have found a partner and autonomously decided to abandon the maternal home. Two separations, two irreversible abandonments. The first from the womb, then the other, from the nest of her home. She was aware that it was a stupid thought, but she often found herself mourning the perspective of seeing the baby grow up. Only the idea of it filled her with sadness.

Then one day, while she was grocery shopping at the mall, she witnessed a terrible event. A woman had lost her son. They had called his name over the intercom, without result. The announcement had been repeated on a regular basis for more than one hour, but the child wasn't found. Police had been alerted, and the mall security searched the place for some time, but with no results. The boy seemed to have disappeared into thin air. Rumour was starting to spread that someone had "taken him". A small clutch of people was trying to support the shattered mother, who sat, catatonic, on a chair. Tears had by then dried on her blank face, leaving black smears of make-up. Paula pitied that woman, and most of all, her instincts were buzzing from the possibility that one day something like this could happen to her too. She pictured herself in that face streaked by drooling anguish, powerlessly facing the countless wolves lying in wait in the forest of life that could have separated her from her child. The episode persuaded her even more that she wouldn't have let anything, or anyone take her child away from her.

The first time she dared to express her feelings with Ned, they were having breakfast. He kept on blabbering about the best way to arrange the nursery, and the possibility of hiring a babysitter; she had raised her gaze from her plate and said dreamily.

"I want to keep her."

"We are surely going to keep her," Ned laughed. "Or have we been working so hard to give her away?"

"You don't get it. I want to keep her inside me."

Ned stared at her as if it was the cup speaking.

"What are you talking about, Paula? Have you gone crazy?"

She didn't think she had gone crazy at all. She serenely explained to him the reasons that led her to that decision, that was, as she announced top him, unshakable. She wanted the baby to grow in her belly. While talking, she looked absolutely convinced about what she was saying, as if it was up to her, another way to end the event with a logical conclusion.

Her husband blamed the entire issue on a hallucinatory delusion of some sort due to hormonal imbalance and didn't mention it again. He adopted the strategy of silence every time Paula brought up the subject. The third trimester of her pregnancy was coming to an end, and once Paula delivered, all those fantasies would have been just a faded memory.

But the last term came and went, without any changes. The average delay that comes with a first pregnancy alarmingly stretched over time. On Ned's insistence, the gynaecologist was consulted, and after a series of complicated pondering that involved the participation of her colleagues, the doctor claimed that there weren't any conditions to induce labour. It looked as if the baby was simply in denial. She needed more time. While leaving the doctor's office, Ned got the feeling that even she didn't know what was going on, and the thought filled him with anger.

There was crying, yelling, doors slammed. Ned felt as if he had stumbled into a condition of illogical insanity, and came to think that Paula - whose natural mystic attitude and curiosity towards occult practices, he had always tried to subdue in favor of more scientific and reasoned arguments – had performed who knew what foul or wacky ritual upon herself, just to get what she wanted. Nature hadn't supplied him with the primogenital strength of a mother defending her child and couldn't believe that Paula had seriously been able to dictate such power over her own body with the sole force of will. He became afraid to touch his wife. The first time he heard the baby crying, during one of their frequent fights, he thought he had fallen prey to another horrendous fantasy. But the wail was repeated, muffled by the womb, and it was clear and real, and Ned was struck by a powerful nausea that traveled through him from head to toe, and he was forced to sit down. When Paula, during her twelfth month of that surreal condition, let him hear the articulated little verses the baby made - and he could hear them, by god he heard them, through that layer of swollen and taut like a drum skin – he almost went mad.

At the twenty-fourth month of pregnancy, Ned packed his things and left the house. In the course of those long, endless months he had tried in every possible way to get used to Paula's condition, to force himself to understand her, but he couldn't do it. The whole matter seemed to him so unfair and unnatural, causing him to perpetually live in a condition of searing resentment, and this had irreparably polluted their relationship. Paula comforted herself as best she could, basking in the presence of her child. Melanie somersaulted in her belly and laughed. She blew bursting bubbles with her mouth. Paula kindly scolded her if she distracted her while she was working, and intimately smiled, feeling like the only person aware of a big, sweet secret. Thanks to her daughter, she rediscovered the pleasure of watching cartoons, reading picture books, going on the swing, albeit the other mothers taking their children to the park looked at her a bit bewildered due to her condition, and were frightened when Melanie screamed for her to go faster. Paula felt that she was learning again, because of her. Melanie experienced life through Paula's senses. Paula, thanks to her, saw things in a different light.

Paula observed the mothers at the park calling to their children, repeatedly summoning them when they didn't obey, panicking if they moved too far away, comforting them when they tripped on their own feet and found themselves on the ground in tears, trying to control their worries when cuts bled too profusely, when the child wasn't in sight and wasn't responding to their call, when the child's arm hurt and was bent in a strange angle after falling from their bike. She observed all of this and caressed her own belly, calm, grateful that she would not have to experience those kind of episodes, that all that was buffered by the protective shell of her belly, dissolved in the quiet stagnation of the amniotic fluid that no external agent could have endangered, because it was part of her.

"Mommy, I can't sleep!" Melanie whimpered at night, in a tearful voice. "It's dark! I had a bad dream!"

"Honey," Paula replied, touched, "that was just a stupid nightmare. It's okay. You are in Mommy's belly. Nothing bad can ever happen to you. Try to get some sleep."

"But it's too dark," the child complained, "couldn't you leave a light on? Just to know it is there? Please!"

Paula raised herself up on her elbows, moved by that helpless little voice.

"All right. There you go, I have turned on the lamp by my bedside. Now go night-night, okay?"

Melanie thanked her, wished her goodnight, and Paula felt her rocking by herself in her womb. Since that night and many more, Paula learnt to sleep face-turned to the other side of the room, the lamp throwing a shadow cone on the wall, until Melanie felt courageous enough to give up the light. With the passage of time, their relationship strengthened more and more, and transformed, following the passing of the years. Melanie went with mommy to work, and knew she had to stay quiet. They went shopping, and she gave Paula her opinion on which dress to buy, something comfortable for both and not too tight across the belly. They chose which movie to catch at the cinema, or the flavor of ice-cream to lick while walking through the park, commenting on scenes of everyday life.

"Which one would you go out with, the blonde or the dark haired one?" her daughter asked her one night, while watching a teen-drama on TV.

"I don't know, which one do you like best?" Paula wanted to find out, amused.

"Both of them. I'd go out with one first, then the other. No, with both of them together, at the same time."

"Mel! that's not ok!"

"Why? It's not that I'd tell them! I'd make sure they wouldn't know."

"It's not fair to them," Paula reprimanded in a severe tone. "Would you like that, if the boys tricked you that way?"

"It's just for fun!" Melanie replied, with a joyful laugh.

Paula fell silent, but she inwardly thought she would impart on her daughter some more lessons on tenderness in a relationship. She and Ned had spent seventeen years of love and mutual respect together.

Later, when the movie ended, Paula turned off the TV and got ready for bed, but Melanie threw a tantrum. She absolutely wanted to stay up late and watch another episode, and she was moving heavily on purpose to prevent her mother from going to sleep.

"No," said Paula firmly.

Melanie threw a blitz of punches against the wall of the uterus, screaming.

As time passed, the sweet and curious child that she was, turned irritable and short-tempered. She was no longer subjected to her mother's will, and when they were at odds with one another, she strenuously fought until she got what she wanted. She caused her mother nausea, she bombarded her belly with vicious kicks, taking her breath away and preventing her from walking. Paula was obliged to indulge her most ridiculous requests to avoid incurring the physical repercussion. With fear, she started to realise that she had lost control over the child, and with that, control over her own body.

Since Melanie had acquired the skill to recognise and repeat, Paula had always been careful to measure her words, to carefully select TV programmes to avoid passing on to her anything too violent, but just the same, her daughter had started cursing like a sailor, and she sometimes seemed to be pleased with her own belligerency, giving in to profanities with gusto.

The movies Paula watched on TV had no appeal to her, and she forced her mother to change the channel until she found something that pleased her, that usually included gore and a large amount of bloodshed. She wanted to listen to music Paula didn't understand, and of which she was somehow afraid of. Melanie rejected any kind of melody, preferring noise instead. The more, the better. The more the words seemed a painful regurgitation, the better. She despised Paula's singer and song proposals and made a fuss, insulting and criticising until her mother put on something she liked. Paula remained in silence, drums hammering in her ears and the electric guitar's suffering screech sawing something right at the centre of her throat, the enthusiasm with which her daughter reacted to that noise shaking her belly so hard she feared it would have broken off. And she asked herself, with an increasing worriedness, if her daughter was crazy. She tried to ask her why she liked that racket so much, and she laconically replied it burned off all the anger she felt. Paula had tried to investigate the cause of that anger, which in her view had no explanation, she had always been such a calm person! But she had never been able to get to the bottom of the situation.

One night, at about 1.30, Paula was awakened by a series of dull thumping on the inside of her belly.

"Hey! Hey!"

"What is it?"

"I can't sleep."

"Every day I tell you to wake up earlier in the morning. If you don't open your eyes before two o' clock in the afternoon, you'll never be able to get to sleep at a decent hour."

"Don't bust my balls," Melanie rudely replied. "I'm nervous. I have to calm down. I need a smoke."

Paula straightened up in bed, suddenly wide awake.

"What?!"

"You heard me, I told you I crave nicotine. I have this itch and it won't go away, and it's exactly *that* need. You did it too, even if you haven't smoked in twenty years. You have it inside you. You gave me the craving, and now you have to satisfy me."

At 2.34 in the morning, wearing her pajamas under her coat, Paula was forced to go the first vending machine to purchase a pack of twenty. This scene was repeated several times. Paula had never been a smoker, except for an occasional cigarette with her high school friends, and she surely wouldn't have accepted her sixteen-year-old daughter to become a slave to smoking, a bad habit and harbinger of something worse. But Melanie showed no quarter, and she found herself with an irresistible urge, foreign to her and yet required to be satisfied. Paula felt so ashamed every time she went grocery shopping and always had to add alcoholic drinks to her cart or go to the store to buy cigarettes. She was subjected to the scolding glances of the cashiers pointed towards her delicate condition, and she always felt the need to justify herself, to explain her purchases were for a third person. After all, there was no way to refuse. Melanie liked to drink, and she immediately noticed if the beer her mother had bought was alcohol-free, and in that way she was, in Melanie's opinion, 'trying to screw' her.

At the office, to give logical explanation to that strange phenomenon that was Paula, her colleagues took to saying that she just hadn't lost her pregnancy weight, or that she was just fat. Nevertheless, she was a beautiful woman, radiant - although a little worn out, lately - and was able to endear herself to others.

One morning Phillip, her cubicle neighbour, after months of silent devotion finally had the courage to ask her out. He had noticed that Paula wasn't wearing a wedding ring since time immemorial. Phillip was almost bald, he wore old-fashioned horn-rimmed spectacles and had a little middle age spread pushing his shirt out, but he was smart and kind, with a great sense of humor. Moreover, Paula hadn't gone on a date in literally ages. She was flattered by it and accepted.

"Why are you getting all dressed up?" Melanie asked that fateful evening, while Paula was getting ready in front of the mirror.

Since she had the habit of being dead to the world until late in the morning, she presumably had missed the proposal.

"We've been invited to dinner, tonight," Paula announced, adjusting an earring.

She had regained a sense of euphoria that had been dead for years, and she was perfectly playing the role of one of those American movie mothers who open up to their teenage daughters.

"I have a date with a man."

"Oh, yeah?" Melanie commented without enthusiasm. "It wouldn't happen to be my douche bag of a father, would it?"

For some time, Ned had reappeared in Paula's life. He practically had come out of nowhere and had pleaded with her to go out for a coffee with him. Paula had accepted. Ned looked pale, and a bit thinner. They had a long chat. He was living with another woman now, several years younger than him. He recently had a son. This event had made him think about how selfish he'd been years ago, towards Paula and his never born daughter. He declared to be terribly sorry to have left the scene, but he did it because he was afraid of how unnatural that whole situation was. He didn't understand the motivations that had pushed Paula to make that gesture, and he still didn't get them. But he claimed it had been unfair on his part to disappear like that, burdening Paula with the expenses of the apartment they rented together. He wasn't asking her to get back together, because he just couldn't handle it. He was in love with another woman, and he still didn't share Paula's decision, and he never would. But even though he wouldn't have been able to stay by her side as before, he wanted to be there in her moments of need. Melanie was his child, as much as his new son. He made a mistake. Could Paula forgive him?

They parted with a hug and remained on good terms.

This had happened about four years ago. Since then, Ned had called every now and then on the phone, and, although never speaking directly to her, he always asked about the little girl. Melanie, who was thirteen at the time and had always lived without a father, had refused to have a relationship of any kind with him. Paula knew she was suffering with abandonment issues, and she didn't accept a stranger suddenly wanting to be a father to her. Over the years, this rejection had turned to full-fledged resentment. Melanie couldn't stand him. Every time she talked about her father, she depicted him as a 'wanker' or a 'douche bag', or, preferably, a 'casual dispensary of semen' who distractedly impregnated women.

Paula reassured her it wasn't Ned, but a guy from her office. At the beginning, Melanie made a fuss because there was a TV programme she was interested in, but after a couple of elbow strikes, she oddly gave in, closing herself in a sulky mutism. Paula perceived that she was actually thrilled by the perspective of a date, because it was something she never did, and she was curious to know what it was like.

Phillip was right on time. He took her to eat at an Italian restaurant. They drank a lot of wine, and overall, they had a pleasant evening. Paula always introduced herself to everyone as an average single mother with an average teenage daughter. She had given up explaining her bizarre situation years ago. She had tried, some time before, when her office colleagues who had distractedly followed her pregnancy saw her scurrying around, still carrying her great belly, and they stopped her in the hallways between the cubicles to exclaim:

"Paula, haven't you delivered yet? I thought your term had ended!"

She happily replied:

"I know, but I loved her so much I decided to keep her inside!" An affirmation to which, in return, usually got a laugh, or a polite puzzled glance.

She had adopted the same strategy when once a saleswoman at a clothing store had approached her smiling, and sweetly asked her:

"What an amazing baby bump you have! May I ask, how many months are you?" And Paula, with the same courtesy, had turned to her and replied: "Oh, about five years!"

The saleswoman had walked away with a horrified expression.

Since then, Paula always acted like Melanie was a physical identity separate from her, living a life of her own. All of this had implicated making up a huge amount of those that Paula defined 'little white lies', not so much related to Melanie's tastes, that manifested pretty clearly from the beginning, but regarding the school she attended, her extracurricular activities, her social life, her relationship with technology. It was a path fraught with more pitfalls then Paula had ever imagined, and she found herself to act as vaguely as possible, when she talked about her daughter, because it wasn't a true life, just a fantasised one. She still remembered when she had made up a story about some swimming club minibus that came to pick Melanie up right after school – to justify how she managed to raise a child alone while working a full-time job, and one of her colleagues had replied:

"My daughter takes the same bus as well! It's so strange they haven't met!"

Paula had felt her blood running cold.

Throughout the evening, even Phillip had asked her a lot of questions about Melanie, thinking to please her. After all, parents always like to talk about their children.

"How's your daughter doing? Does she do her homework? Is she a good student?"

Paula dazzlingly said something about Melanie attending an industrial technical institute and being at the top of her class. She stirred on a familiar territory, confiding to Phillip that she was worried lately, because Melanie liked to drink and smoke. Phillip had reacted with an indulgent smile.

"It's typical. She's sixteen."

Driven by the comfort of the wine, Paula came to confess that she was afraid her daughter could hurt herself during what Philip defined as 'the emotional turmoil of the teenage years'. Leaning on Phillip, she whispered in his ear that she feared the harm those tendencies could have on her, to Paula herself.

Phillip tried to soothe that excessive concern explaining that there was nothing to be worried about. He believed it to be perfectly normal being lured by a certain kind of 'forbidden fruit', at that age. He tenderly added that, that in his humble opinion, part of Melanie's turmoil was due to the lack of a fatherly figure in her life. He said that in a moved voice, taking Paula's hand in his own, and sweetly caressing her ringless finger.

Later, he escorted her home and departed after a sweaty moustache brushing kiss. The gesture left Paula with a pleasant feeling of heat in her groin. She was just about to invite him up, but at the last minute restrained herself. It didn't seem fair to Melanie, nor appropriate for her daughter to see her in certain circumstances. Therefore, she suffocated her instincts. But Melanie, quiet until then, intoxicated by the wine, suddenly jerked awake by the arousal that had rekindled her mother's senses.

"Hey! OH!" she called to her, pushing her hands on the belly. "So what's going on? Is it over already, that's how it ended? That's all of our Casanova's sex drive?"

"Melanie," Paula kindly scolded her, leaning on the chest of drawers, "there's no other way it should have ended."

She had resumed the confidential tone of the American mother, trying to recover that complicity that her daughter denied her, turning to her with an aggression and a roughness that was suited more to the basements of certain English slums rather than to a delightful cottage in the suburbs of Los Angeles.

"Why? Why didn't he bang you?"

"For a thousand times, don't use that horrible expression. He didn't have to do anything. We went out for dinner, and we spent a pleasant evening as friends. Maybe next time we'll go for a coffee, and..."

"And wait for cobwebs to grow down there?" Melanie scornfully interrupted her. "Come on, don't tell me that you've already hung your cunt on a nail, at your age!"

Paula was speechless. She felt an urgency releasing from her belly, from her daughter's hungry words, which frightened her. A craving that perhaps even exceeded the appetite Melanie had shown for junk food, alcohol and nicotine.

"Call him back, mom. Maybe it's not too late and he'll come back straight away. No, actually, let's find another one. Let's find ourselves another one, mom, one we like more, not this second-hand guy, one with a nice cock, who knows how to use it properly, a horse-sized cock that he can stick all the way up, all the way, the way we like it..."

Paula couldn't stop that heavy outpouring of aroused words that mortified her, and she let out a scream, slamming her fist on the chest of drawers.

"Enough!"

She didn't even know from where in her all that authority had climbed back. Maybe it had something to do with her hormonal turmoil, or the upset state of her womb. The flow of words broke off.

"We won't do anything. We won't call anybody, and we won't go anywhere. Now. It's time. To go. TO SLEEP!" Paula roared, throwing the jewelry box on the ground in rage.

The object broke in half with the sharp crack of a slap.

There was a moment of silence, long enough to allow Paula to be attacked by doubt permeated by regret. Then Melanie delivered a tremendous blow to her belly that made her fall forward, and if she hadn't promptly protected with her hands, she would have banged her face on the floor. For a moment, Paula saw black. Melanie's voice came trembling from the womb, every syllable bloated, full of venom.

"I want to fuck, all right? And not with one of those sixty-year-old limp dicks you hang out with, I want a boy, a boy the way I like them, and I swear to god," and to be sure to be sufficiently understood, she pounded against her mother's belly once more, "I won't leave you alone until you do what I say."

Paula tightened her coat around her, mascara running down her cheeks. Her heels produced a sinister echo on the concrete. The area was badly lit, garbage overflowing from the bins. Every shadow startled her. She had to do everything quickly, she hadn't even had time to change. Dressed like that, more fitting for dinner in a sophisticated downtown restaurant than for a walk alone at such a late hour in the inner city, she felt even less respectable, in danger. The front door was located on a side street. Paula buzzed the squalid intercom, and immediately a counterfeit male voice answered, directing her to the third floor. The stairs were cramped and narrow, with worn steps. There was no elevator. Climbing up, Paula bumped against a man wearing a hat and a turquoise scarf who was coming down the stairs, minding his own business, and she was so frightened that she almost tripped on a step and risked tumbling down the entire flight. Zack was standing in the doorway, nervously biting the inside of his cheek. Paula had fished him in a casual dating chat site in a fetish room reserved for 'peculiar passions', Melanie had chosen him. He was in his 20s, and handsome in his own way, he had a strange, almost alien appeal. His face was partly disfigured by a residual of juvenile acne on his forehead. He was blond and lanky, and he proved to be good-mannered and delightfully nervous. He walked her into his dirty apartment. He had her sit at the small table in a suffocating kitchenette and offered her something to drink. They chatted for a bit, and Paula learned that Zack was an apprentice carpenter. He earned just enough to be able to afford that little apartment, and he was proud not to depend on his family. His family didn't have a lot of money, and he had four sisters. In his spare time, he went to his friends' gigs. He struggled to find a girlfriend because of his 'peculiar passion', he had always liked pregnant women, and he ended up to losing interest in girls who weren't. Sometimes it was hard, it caused him problems. What about her? Did she still live with the baby's father? And what did she like to do? Paula was nearly starting to feel at ease, and for a moment it was like she was talking to a nephew or a school student, an almost comfortable sensation. But then, when the time came to get down to business, everything precipitated into darkness again. She simply didn't want to have sex with him. Obviously, Melanie wasn't on the same page, and Zack lacked the sensitivity and experience to realise something was wrong. He positioned her on all fours on the bed, and whispered in her ear:

"You're a cow, a pregnant cow, now moo for me."

Paula burned with shame, stunned. But Zack wouldn't cut her slack. He squeezed her breasts until it hurt, deliriously babbling he would have liked to see her squirting milk. He kept on addressing her with obscenities, defining her with derogatory remarks that embarrassed her, until he managed to come. Anyway, he was attentive to deal blows with vigorous but not alarming force, and he kept on rubbing his hands on the taut belly. It seemed it was one of the things that attracted him the most, and it was immediately clear to Paula why Melanie's choice had fallen on him. It was so sleazy and sick. Staring at the headboard getting closer and then withdrawing to the rhythm of every thrust, her face reduced to an inflamed mask and the sense of oppression of being forced, steeling her body, Paula said to herself this was the last straw.

The next morning, she felt like a thief. Melanie was satisfied for the moment, but Paula knew she would soon awaken, and she was aware that she wouldn't be able to contain anymore, the destructive power released by her daughter. She needed to get rid of her, to expel her from the peaceful oasis of her uterus before it turned into a battlefield.

Profiting of her daughter's unhealthy sleeping habits, she started a frantic tour of clinics. None of the hospitals she turned to, gave consent for the abortion pill, because at the sight of her swollen belly they declared it was too late, and she could have caused irreversible damage. It was forbidden by law. It was simply cruel. At that stage, it wasn't possible to have an abortion anymore. Paula had stopped going to the gynecologist after the twelfth month she had kept the baby inside, so her case had no longer been monitored, and it was lost among the hundreds of others who in seventeen years had strolled through those rooms carrying a life inside themselves. A couple of times, she had tried to explain the situation to the doctors and nurses, but she obviously obtained the sole result of looking like a lunatic. Nobody was willing to believe that inside her something had been growing for such a long time.

When psychiatric treatment turned out to be a concrete possibility, embodied by a conscientious objector doctor, Paula gave up on seeking help.

So, she retrieved a phone number that she had gotten online a long time ago and visited the witch doctor she had consulted years before. That woman was the only person who believed her. She talked to Paula about destructive demons and other evil entities, and she performed a ritual on her. Eventually, she handed her a concoction of herbs to drink right away, and she assured her that, through certain trades among people she knew, and whose names it was better not to pronounce, she would supply Paula with what she needed.

Two days went by, and Paula was eaten alive by the anguish that Melanie, due to the osmotic binding connecting the two of them, despite all of her precautions would have started to sense something was wrong, and would have decided to dispose of her first, to avoid coming to a bad end.

During the following appointment, the witch doctor had given Paula three different pills which would have given her a stomach ache but would help her expel Melanie from her uterus. Paula was unaware that some of those pills were used by veterinarians to cause dogs to miscarry. The woman pleaded with her not to exaggerate the dosage, but Paula was so desperate, she wasn't able to comply with the requirements.

As soon as Paula had taken one pill, after the first annoyed grumbling, Melanie understood what was going on, but she couldn't do anything to stop it. She kept on howling excruciatingly, a heavy downpour of horrible, dirty insults, punctuated by cries and the tearing shrieks of a pig in a slaughterhouse. Paula popped pills after pills. Her belly was shaking as if a war was raging inside of it. It seemed Melanie was determined to break her down, judging from the violence of her assaults. Slowly, the effects of that killer cocktail began to manifest. Paula agonised on her bed, plagued by atrocious spasms that made her delirious. The most horrible sensation was feeling her baby melting in the fire of her burning guts, that seemed to eat themselves from the inside, their pulp gnawed by a myriad of swarming creatures like worms digging tunnels in apples. She could hear her daughter cursing her, consuming herself in pain, and it felt like she was fighting to get out of that furnace in which she was trapped, that was serving her the coupe the grace. Paula's body contracted and stretched to its limit, attempting to expel its contents, and she heard Melanie writhing in her belly, continually painfully yelling: "What did you do to me, mommy, what did you do to me!"

"I'm doing it for you, baby! I'm doing it for you!" Paula screamed, pushing with every contraction.

The next morning, after having called several times without receiving any answer, Ned showed up at his old house, opening the door with his keys. He needed to speak to Paula about some papers pertaining to the separation they both had mutually decided to.

He found her supine, lying on her bed.

From her belly, ripped apart, a short, rotten plant sprouted balefully, gnarled and rooted on itself, slick from the blood that still soaked its knobby roots, and greasy with a yellow, gluey substance that trickled down the extremities of two sharp branches, hooked like claws.

# THE BREEDING

At the time, we lived in a house by the seaside. Ours wasn't a wealthy family, only my father had a job. My mother took care of the house and my numerous younger siblings. My father worked in the meat industry, the meat that comes from the sea. He worked in the fish canning factory that was much further away, in the countryside, too far to reach by bike, that's why we never went to visit him.

The factory had been built about fifteen years earlier, decided by individuals belonging to the higher classes of society, too high to go through the trouble of communicating their intentions to the locals. Overnight, the unaware inhabitants saw parading in front of their eyes a procession of trucks, cranes, forklifts, containers. In the scorching, stunned heat of summer, the construction site had been erected bit by bit. And with it, arrived the prohibitions. No fishing after so many miles offshore; since that moment, deep waters was under the control of the big corporation that had started the building site, where a factory was to be constructed. The company would not only process the fish, but also fish the very same. No swimming or boating too far out, for the same reason; it was trespassing. Several signs appeared in town, each one indicating the portions of the beach where it was still allowed to own a business renting boats; some moorings were now the property of the factory owners, as well. Without asking us, hands more elegant than ours had little by little mapped the land, and shared the water among themselves.

Once completed, the factory was the size of a gargantuan mammoth in a field where crops were once planted. A gigantic, ugly barracks-like building with large doors and windows narrow like slits, huge tanks were connected to pipes and smoke-stacks from which spouted thick and pestilential black smoke. Its outline could be seen from afar, against the cultivated acres, its dark shape breaking the horizon when, at dawn, you turned your gaze towards it, covering your eyes with your hands.

And yet, it was thanks to that mysterious monster of metal and concrete, that our little town prospered. Ours had been for decades a fishing community. Although at first the building of that enormous complex had caused more than a little dissatisfaction among the fishermen, whose livelihoods had been taken away, soon the factory had created hundreds of jobs, and since it was more profitable to work there, the fishermen had turned into factory workers. My father was one of them.

For me, the eldest child, I knew that after that spring my childish days of playing would be over, and I was destined to take my place in the factory, hopefully as a book keeper, like my father, who had studied a few more numbers than the others and because of that worked for twelve hours a day in the comfort of an office, and not in the machine rooms or the processing lines. Thanks to a friend of his, in charge of canning, who sometimes secretly gave him unregistered cans of fish, my father managed to snag home a little extra. In the evening, when he opened the worn door of our single-story cottage and pulled from the lining of his coat two or three aluminum cans with the big company trademark printed on them, in red and blue ink, the evening turned festive. While we raced to set the table for dinner, my mother opened the cans with care, harpooning out with a fork pieces of grey and pink meat immersed in a liquid of preservatives. She laid it, dripping and juicy, on our plates. It was savoury, with a spicy aftertaste that left a salty, pleasant halo on the tip of your tongue. The flavour was new, bizarre, never savoured before, it tasted exotic. This special taste had conquered the palates of all the towns inhabitants. Fish like that, was nowhere to be found. Its quality was renowned throughout the whole province. Those cans ended up on the tables of the most fashionable restaurants on the mainland, on the tables of the wealthy and noble. It was considered a delicacy, and it sold for a high price. For the poorer, was left over the lowest quality fish, that which the families caught on their own from their small boats, in the authorised zone, never going too far from the shore.

All the fish arriving on the tables of the wealthiest came from the humongous breeding farm that I found myself observing every day from the coast. It had been set up more or less at the same as the factory, by the same owners. I have the faintest memory of that time, as I was very young. I remember the boats and trawlers offshore, but most of all I remember a small, tiny dot that gradually grew bigger, we were allowed to observe that construction only from a distance. Moving closer was strictly forbidden, my father used to say because it was out in the open sea, and it was dangerous. We suspected the real reason was, instead, a ruse by the owners of the plant, who didn't want intruders at the property in fear they would steal some fish. The breeding constituted an inaccessible mystery to us, and like all mysteries was soaked by the special fascination of things that are forbidden. We often found ourselves sitting on the sand, staring at those far, indistinct spots, and conjecturing upon their nature, on the material they were built of. Pretty soon, I became obsessed with it. I've always felt inside me the call to adventure, which I satisfied with explorations along the coast with my peers, combined with an attraction for the sea that was so strong as to lead my mother to consider it unhealthy. Like many other boys, I dreamed of sailing the sea, that sea so familiar to me, that very sea I had frequented during lazy, milky dawns, waiting to see the fishing nets stretching, in the starry nights when it merged with the sky, in my daily swims to the red buoys marking the forbidden area, beyond which gigantic yellow signs decorated with menacing symbols and erected on floats, ordained that it was forbidden to trespass. We often had races swimming to the buoys, holding onto the floats squeezing our eyes, trying to catch any invisible details through salt-encrusted eyelashes. Soon, I started racing there by myself, pushing myself to that border, alone. My friends, despite having curiosity about the plant, didn't share the same craving for the water as I did, the attachment to that blue, iridescent mass that confused me.

I soon started adjusting my moods to those of the sea. This sense of harmony seemed to me a trait shared by all the members of the village. The menstrual cycles of the women were regulated by the slow rising and lowering of the tides, a motion like their behavior, when they let themselves be chased, offering themselves. During summer nights, the sky was lit by luminous trails breaking far away, out at sea, and we children would watch them while lying on the sand, tracing their descent with our fingers. Legend had it, that those lights were the same starfish which profusely appeared on the beach the next day, stars that we picked up by the armfuls. When masses of clouds gathered in the sky, and the sea became chaotic, it rose like a restless horse on two legs, shaking its mane, breaking upon itself. I used to sit on the shore at a safe distance, during those days grey with clouds, when the sea turned black and rippled, and rose, swollen with a violent turmoil, a warning to stay away, that it wanted to be left alone, and angrily discharged threatening waves on the shore, sucking into a vortex that part of itself that it had just spat on the sand, like an abusive man holds his lover after beating her in the course of a violent fight. I sat there, satisfying myself with the spray that rained upon me from that passionate fury, with the few drops of water I was allowed to receive, asking myself what secrets the sea was keeping, and what was agitating in its bowels. During those days, I stared at the breeding farm, far, silent, and swaying, I questioned myself on the fate of its occupants in those instances of battle.

Days after the storm, having cooled its anger, the sea brought us gifts, like a regretful lover after a fit of jealousy. Scales, plastic, parts of boats, frayed shreds of clothing. There was always something new, unseen and useful.

We laced shell bracelets, and I wondered.

In those serene days, the green-streaked water shone as if it contained precious stones to be caught by the handful. I looked at the placid coming and going of the tide, those slight swinging motions, almost hoping to be swallowed by it. The lazy bending of the waves, its separating from its primitive matter, its curling and again merging into itself, becoming one with the substance that generated it, the salt air filling my nostrils with a sharp, irresistible scent. I squeezed my eyes wounded by the dazzling surface that sparkled like an expanse of diamonds, and my gaze inevitably landed on that area in which gibbous shapes rocked, inarticulate and indistinct, in a place where the sea seemed to darken, almost locked, like a treasure chest.

It was this obsession of mine that pushed me to take a step that was often the subject of discussion between me and my friends, but that nobody had ever dared to do. Crossing past the red buoy border, going as far as the breeding farm itself. Together, we had built a little rowboat, with which we sailed in small adventures along the coast, to hidden coves, returning laden with cockles. I explained my plan to my crew, but they, after the initial exclamations of longing, had clearly refused. Most of them feared the consequences of being seized by those in charge of guarding the breeding farm. They were afraid of the fist of the law, of being severely punished for their reckless actions, for their harmless curiosity. We understood, when it came to business, there was no place for compassion or understanding.

There was also another reason lingering in the air among the village inhabitants, a concept well-known to each one of us, that my father used to repeat like an admonishment, in a serious tone. That the sea does not forgive, and it can be merciless when it feels you're not paying it respect. But I felt protected by the armor of certainty that this didn't apply to me. I felt a total symbiosis with the sea, I was conscious of being a child generated by it, and it would have never betrayed me. I listened to the sound of the backwash that for me had always been a lullaby and lured me like the song of the Sirens. There was something irresistibly alluring in the sea and the secrets it held.

My friends and my brothers soon grew tired of what they considered the ravings of a fanatic, and they tried to dissuade me from my plan of adventure using mockery and judicious reasoning. But each passing day I spent with that transparent water lapping my limbs, with every stroke along the shoreline, I intimately reinforced my intentions.

I chose a sunny and warm afternoon, conscious of the reflection of the light on the waves that would have been my ally, concealing me from sight. White, bloated clouds piled up on the horizon. I calculated it wouldn't have been a problem, I felt safe protected by the strong and osmotic bonding the water transmitted to me.

It was lunchtime, an inconvenient time for fishing, families were gathered around a poor meal. I headed out, on the pretext of taking my usual swim.

I dragged our little rowboat out of the cave where we had hidden it, I set sail. There wasn't a living soul around, I felt like I was the only inhabitant of the village. The sea under my hull was the sole, silent witness of my undertaking. I was wearing my usual light-blue swimsuit, faded from wear and tear, and I had with me my mask and snorkel that I had brought along out of precaution, uncertain of what I would have found. I rowed effortlessly towards the gigantic yellow signs, swaying lazily, standing out against the sky with their sinister threat. I shipped the oars and lowered a small weight tied to a rope to keep the boat anchored there. To prying eyes, it would have looked like the someone had stopped to fish or swim in that spot, where it was still permitted to do so, and they wouldn't have thought anything was out of place.

From there, I would swim, head below the surface, barely visible on the slight rising of the waves, it would be difficult to single me out. While I put on my flippers, I noticed the wind had picked up a bit. My calculations were wrong, the mattress of clouds had swiftly become thicker and had expanded, a sign they were closing rapidly. From its farthest spot, the sky was closing in. Even the sea seemed to have darkened. I considered going back, but I told myself I couldn't miss this opportunity. I stared at the water. It returned the stare, invitingly, it seemed to me almost expectantly. It was that knowing look that made me decide to continue my adventure, before hesitation dug doubt inside of me, I dove into the blue.

Immediately at ease, I made the second mistake of that day. Never having ventured past the border, I'd been able to just guess at the distance between me and the breeding farm, which, from my position, seemed much closer than it really was. To reach the first underwater pillar that supported the plant, it took me at least twice as long as foreseen. Under the surface, the water was so thick it was like a wall, I stopped. The right direction was not clear to me, I couldn't see what was around me, it all appeared the same to me. I only knew that to reach my goal, I had to keep going straight, just now I can say for certain that should have been a warning. At the time I was stubborn, pig-headed, focused on the target. I kept going. I arrived with no strength, worn out. I held on to the concrete pillar hiding behind its imposing form to regain my breath.

In front of me, opened a post-apocalyptic scenario. Dozens and dozens of pillars like the one I was grasping, were placed at equal distances from each other and were repeated for miles. I studied the concrete cylinder I hid behind. It was encrusted with shells and algae, strapped with a yellow float where at the water's surface and covered with rusty ropes, yellowed dried by the sun. I tried to plunge under, but I immediately lost my breath. The surroundings, not very clear, didn't help my breathing. I tried again, going down a little lower. My mask became obscured by white strands of mucus.

I realised that deep down, where the pressure wouldn't have allowed me to sink to, the ropes tied to the pillar supported nets crammed with fish. The water there had a strange quality, viscous, black, almost oily. It must have been the result of the waste products of hundreds of organisms swimming several feet below me. I was under the impression that I would have emerged from that swim dirtier than before. I sniffed the wind. The air around me had changed. It was dense, stagnating, greenish, veined with a sharp and indefinable smell. It took me a while to realise it smelled like death. A thick mist had risen, white, foamy, blurring the outlines of things. I couldn't see the shoreline anymore, just a milky, murky fog which seemed to get closer, bigger, expanding, eating the sea and merging with the sky.

The ruin of a structure that looked like an enormous, rusty mechanical spider with long legs, lay a few feet from me, bent and abandoned maybe due to the force of the sea. I ignored its function.

The centre of that field cultivated with pillars hosted an undefined number of humongous pens enclosed by nets, in which something was gurgling and literally bubbling. The frenzied activity of the pens occupants was so fast paced that it came to my ears as an insistent buzzing vibration, like an electric spark. It seemed it was that very vibration that generated the small waves lapping over me, languidly caressing me and then departing, leaving me full of longing, as if containing a silent promise.

Unable to resist any longer, I cautiously approached the nearest pen. I anchored myself with my fingers to the mesh dividing me from that burbling vortex. The net was hot. The water was burning.

At first, I wasn't able to catch sight of anything within that infernal activity that was taking place below the net, which lifted a gurgling foam to the waters surface, producing cracking bubbles that burst on me and that, I discovered with astonishment, burned, like lava from a volcano.

I caught a glimpse of a grey flipper, a part of a trunk, a skin fold.

Then suddenly something launched itself so forcefully at the net that it touched my face, and I involuntarily jumped back from the fright, drinking that greasy and turbid water. Everything was confused for an endless moment, I whirled my arms and legs at random, I felt something grab one of my flippers from below, I kicked, I lost it. All around, I perceived the movements of bodies shifting in the water, I hit something which instantly withdrew. I emerged spluttering, hair glued to my face, my lungs burning, contaminated, tangled in seaweed. In front of me, the thing that had thrown itself against the net was slowly sinking downwards, dragged by the underwater vortex.

I saw its livid face, pocked with silver scales, its dribbling mouth opened in a horrible, stupefied 'O', eyes almost lateral, out of proportion, liquid pupils immersed in a dirty-white.

The suffering mask of a woman was being sucked into the turmoil, ripping from her scalp slimy tufts of hair, catching in the mesh of the net, hair with pieces of skin still attached.

The horrified scream that rose to my lips was swallowed by another wave that cruelly slapped me in the face like an icy shower. What I had in front of me was a gigantic carnage of creatures both male and female, of all weight, lengths and age, whose features looked entirely human, if it wasn't for the sick tone of their translucent skin, the yellowish colour at the corner of their mouths, the strange angulation of their lopsided eyes on their long, pointed triangle faces, and most of all their transparent scales, drab and silvery, which covered their bodies which ended in a majestic caudal flipper shining with metallic scales.

The creatures were massed together and followed one another, and each one of them stared at me, some were unconscious, their haggard faces twisted in idiotic grimaces, with bones visible where their scales had come off, shreds of meat and pieces of skin hanging from their necks and cheeks. Others were intact though, eyes alert, darting here and there in alarm. There were hundreds of them, thousands. Sometimes one of those individuals was popped from the crowd like a cork from a bottle, due to the pressure, and would smash against the net, and there would leave fragments of their body before sinking heavily back into the frenzy. Those above, crushed those down below, slapping them with their tails, squashing them under their weight. While those down below struggled not to succumb, it seemed that those above needed to come down from the surface from time to time to swallow draughts of water. The continuous simmering of the water was caused by that constant activity of thousands of wriggling bodies. Eyes mixed with eyes, mouths, flippers.

The most terrible thing was that the scene unfolded in total silence. Agony was expressed by the terror in those darting eyes, in the agitation of their bodies, in the painful, freakish grimaces on their faces. It was clear that those creatures, whatever was their way of expression and communication, couldn't emit a sound. Not a breath came from those crooked mouths, open wide in fear, petrified facial expressions of someone screaming, but not able to because of ruined vocal cords.

I stuck my head underwater.

In that muddy broth, putrid with excrement, I noticed that the net sunk down for several miles and disappeared, swallowed by the sea depths. Judging by the mad bubbles, the whirlpools, the turmoil below, I could see, that the net was overflowing with bodies. It must had been one of these creatures who had previously grabbed my flipper.

I surfaced, confused, full of dread. I was amazed they weren't all already dead, boiled alive in that enormous, infernal hot caldron. Suddenly, a pair of bulging, psychotic bug-eyes jumped at me. A hollow, cadaverous face, green, cheeks sunk into a grotesque impression of a skull. In front of me floated the slender body of a female specimen, about my age, who, with a resolute gesture, brought her upper limbs to the level of my hands, exerting pressure on the thin mesh of the net. The texture of her skin was lumpy and oily. The evolution of what I sensed to be an ancient species had turned those that should have been fingers into a thick, cartilaginous membrane, with a hint of bones where knuckles were located on a human hand. Under the eyes, the skin had formed fleshy and heavy sacks, that bounced at every movement. Her pupils were black and liquid, immersed in a pool of unhealthy white. In the transparency of her sick grey skin I could see the dark blue webbing of the arteries branching through her body like a map. I was able to make them out until the armor of scales became too thick. She had long, gluey hair, sticky with the mucus that oozes from marine animals, hair that floated around her, pulled her, hooked her to somebody else in that mad stampede. She must had been losing tufts of it. On her chest, small breasts hung sadly, empty, covered with silvery flakes. Her facial design forced her to keep the jaw stuck in that constant 'O' of idiotic astonishment. Below the lips, wrinkled by water, I glimpsed a small row of sharp teeth. The nose was flat, alien, almost reduced to only nostrils. Although the anomaly of the facial bones had pushed the eyes to a more lateral position than that of humans, and the crazed motion of the pupils as wide as small plates rolling like wild marbles, she was undoubtedly staring at me. I perceived an attempt at connection and the impossibility of communicating in words, the effort stretching out the tendons of her neck, I ascribed it to a silent cry for help.

There was no need to express it with words, I could clearly see it by myself. Those creatures were suffering.

I started. My eyes burned, and my chest was simultaneously gripped in a feeling of oppression as if someone had emptied it using a gimlet.

I tried to force the mesh of the net, but it seemed to be built with a strong alloy. I should have gone and come back with the proper tools. I couldn't widen it at all using just my bare hands, not even an inch. My palms slipped on that slimy mass of meat scraps, mucus and hair. During all of that, I felt the squinting, sidelong glance of that creature falls on me like a responsibility.

The moment I saw the pointy bow of a trawler emerging from behind one of the pillars, it was too late. The instant I noticed it, the enormous craft was already towering over me. I swam backwards in a hurry. The trawler was so silent it seemed as if deserted, and for a wild moment I asked myself if it was. With a metallic roar, two panels opened along the ship's sides and two monstrous mechanical arms ending in pliers, uncoiled, lowered into the pen, hooked the top portion of the net and lifted it from the water. The girl was ripped away from me. One of the creatures plummeted, falling several feet down, and crashed back in the net below, to keep company with the remnants. The creatures were rolled one upon the other like a pile of minced meat, accompanied by the wet sounds of slapping flippers.

A waterfall poured down on me, and I could barely see that gigantic net full of its struggling catch swaying dangerously above me, the mesh impossibly stretched out, and I had a feeling that the net would give way from the weight of the bodies and that bag of human like creatures would have collapsed on me.

It was then, that I noticed the motorboat. It approached with its engine off, and in the commotion, I had not registered its presence at all.

An intense pain exploded in my foot, as if someone had hit me with a rock. I quickly turned around and understand what happened, and underwater the scene was almost surreal. A large hook was plunged into my heel, attached to the end of a thick, transparent line. I was pulled to the opposite side by a force almost ten times stronger than mine. I had been fished. Although I floundered, there was no getting away. They caught me and hoisted me carelessly onto the motorboat, hanging me by my heel like a tuna. head-down, coughing, I spat water. I had lost my mask and snorkel. The sea was gun-metal, dirty-ice coloured, cold and sharp like a raw diamond. There was foam in my mouth, in my lungs. The wind was bellowing in my ears. And the ghostly, pearly fog, swallowed every scream, every cry for help. As soon as my wounded foot came in touch with the freezing air, it started stinging and burning horribly, a sensation that the water had diminished. I was miserably dropped to the deck, panting, breath ragged. I couldn't stop coughing, and for a moment I thought I was going to leave a lung there. I rolled onto my belly and vomited several times, transparent, green water. Every retch brought with it a jolt of pain from my wounded foot shooting straight to my brain. I barely had recovered, when I saw several shapes of men standing in a semicircle around me. They were of the same height and build, anonymous, protected by white and bizarre dive suits that made them look like astronauts from the abyss. I realised they were staring at me only because their helmets were turned towards my direction. They remained motionless and taciturn.

I immediately started talking, my voice strained by the water and gagging. I apologised through yelps and moans, making amends for my behavior. I said I was a local. I hastily assured them that I had no intention of stealing anything, I wasn't a smuggler, in fact – I had proof – I didn't carry any tools with me. I explained that I had ventured there out of mere curiosity, that I made a mistake, I knew I shouldn't have trespassed, but I meant no harm. I contradicted myself, first I blabbered that I was aware that I was in a forbidden area, then that I had lost my way and simply found myself there. What scared me the most was their silence. I was expecting an earful, harsh rebukes, requests to show my documents. Threats of being dragged in front of the authorities, jail time, my family being called, of me facing the legal consequences of my gesture. Nothing of the above would have been more terrifying than their silence. They remained quiet, as if waiting for me to finish blathering my confused summation. When I stopped to take a breath, the helmet to my right turned towards his fellows and made the smallest movement, an imperceptible nod. I felt despair crashing down on me.

A prayer slipped from my mouth, a whimper. Two of them stepped out and grabbed me. I screamed. I tried to valiantly wriggle free, but their grasps were as strong as chains. Then, I burst into sobs. Through a veil of tears, I noticed the motorboat had slowly flanked the trawler. Then my strength failed me, all I had left were my prayers. They seized me by the scruff of the neck. I was dragged on my stomach from the boat over the gangway. My mouth formed a moaned and strangled "no, no, no..." everybody seemed to be deaf. Throughout all this, no one spoke to me. At every movement of my legs, the hook seemed to plunge deeper into my heel. It had penetrated without spilling a drop of blood, but it promised to rip the flesh as soon as it would be pulled out. Once on board, I discovered that the trawler wasn't deserted at all. Another dozen white suit crowded the deck. I turned to them, begging, sighing, torn apart, my face a mask of snot. It was like the helmets prevented them from hearing my pleas. Not a hint that they heard me, of perhaps a flash of hesitation in their bodies. Four of them lifted me, hefted my body over their shoulders with no apparent effort, not at all perturbed by my wriggling. They carried me belowdecks, down narrow, damp ladders, the way you would carry a coffin to a funeral. I hit my head and limbs against several corners. In my trashing, I slammed my knee into a bulkhead, causing me to see stars. My screams of pain blended with the roaring of the hoarse, menacing sea. Below decks it was dark. There was a brackish, sour smell of stale humidity, shellfish and sea waste.

My eyes, not used to darkness, employed my other senses to aid my orientation. I heard the sea violently pounding against the sides of the ship, reverberating through the guts of the vessel. I was flung into a dark void, I surprisingly landed on something soft with a heavy, wet sound. I gropingly moved my hands around in search of something that would have given me a hint of my surroundings. I was on all fours and my knees were sliding as if I was on a slope, on a child's slide. A sharp pain to my thumb almost made me lose my balance, I immediately withdrew my hand and for a moment I thought of another hook, but when I brought the thumb to my mouth and sucked the metallic, salty blood, I realised that I had been bitten. My face contorted in a panicked and disgusted grimace, heart hammering in my chest like a wild bird. Eyes now accustomed to the dim light allowed me to see what my other senses had already guessed. They had thrown me in what seemed to be a large wooden box, where, haphazardly piled up one on top of the other as they had previously been in the net, were hoarded the creatures. I groped through the crowd, violently shaken by sobs. I impossibly stretched out my arms, trying to reach the edge of the box that seemed miles away. I attempted to cling to the walls of the box, which were made of smooth wood, without any pike or moldings to serve as a hand hold. I trampled on body organs that protested squashing while I mangled faces and bodies under my feet, using them as a leverage to climb. I fell back breaking my fingernails against the wood, I fell back into the mess below, gripped by despair, in that gelatinous, slippery, moving hoard of obtuse faces, reaching limbs and tails in a mute, desperate struggle. My sobs and the roaring sea the only noises filling the room. The teeming mass of living beings, the suffocating stench of stale air and urine. The absolute silence broken only by the growling water, the dim light, the heat of bodies, the cruel, violent rolling of the ship moving the creatures and making them tumble one upon the other... I fought not to be crushed, I thought I would have died, suffocated by the weight of that subhuman rabble, I thought I would have vomited again, I fainted.

I was awakened by the screeching sound of a door being opened. I tried to open my eyes, but my eyelids were encrusted with dried mucous, glued together with bodily fluids that didn't belong to me. I couldn't see anything besides a blinding light, that hurt my eyes. I didn't feel anything and once again lost my senses. I came to in a place I didn't recognise. My eardrums were raped by metallic cacophonies and dull noises. My mouth was half-opened, pasted with the slimy, throbbing taste of the body it was stuck to, and which I felt pulsating against my lips. I was on the filthy floor of a large, dirty-white room with stained walls.

I immediately realised I was in the bowels of the factory, where the pulp, the mush was pressed and reassembled, where from one substance emerged another one, where presumably something came in alive and left dead.

The windows facing the outside were two black eyes reduced to slits. There was, instead, an internal large window with transparent glass looking on another section of the factory. I could spot other white suits busying themselves around an endless conveyor belt. Mechanical arms dropped down from machinery and planed, drilled and modified the structure of an object, making invisible improvements. An upper level overlooked what appeared to be offices, where swarming figures dressed with shirts bustled around heaps of papers and old calculators with elusive looks on their faces, as if they didn't want to watch, they rarely darted their eyes towards us, and always for a fraction of a second. I was struck by the sight of a man wearing a hat and a turquoise scarf, because of the flashy colour of his clothing, he was impressing a rubber stamp onto a pile of papers, and, due to the situation I was in, I found it to be absolute madness.

Although the rooms were soundproof, the metallic noise of the tools buzzed in my ears. The big room I was in, you could have heard a pin drop, but the smell was screaming. It lingered, a persistent, rotten stench of rancid marrow.

I barely turned my head and was able to get a glimpse of a whirling light to my left, as if a flash had been cast into the air, before pain exploded in my knees, so intense it delivered a jolt of electricity directly to my brain and made my body spasm. The room filled with my screams, and I almost puked again from the pain. One of the white suits was towering over me, brandishing a bludgeon also white, one of those that was used to hit cattle in the head, he had just broken both of my knees. I dragged myself onto my elbows, moaning, trying to keep at least the smallest distance between me and the imposing figure standing above me, but he followed me with indolence, showing not even the slightest sign of alarm. I almost got the feeling that he was getting bored watching me agonising on his dirty floor. When he grew tired of it, I may have covered the space between two tiles. I felt myself being grabbed without effort, under my armpits and loaded onto a set of shoulders like a sack. The arms of the suit clamped down on my tortured legs and prevented me from making any movement.

I was carried into another large room through a folding door, which shut in my face. I felt something warm and wet dripping on my lips and I realised the door had split my nose. The pain in my face almost dulled the one in my legs. A new room, new large window, new upper floor, new anonymous faces beaming with sweat, pretending nothing was happening. Among the dozens of confused features following one after another behind the big window, I thought I saw the face of my father, ashen, terrified.

In this large, new room, the clattering of the tools suddenly became real and concrete. I was in the first section of a gigantic assembly line that started when a swaying body was lowered from a hook and placed on the belt, where a white suit cut off its head with an axe before leaving it to the machines, which deprived it of its limbs. The body's trunk was divided into sections, bony parts ripped out and the soft tender meat preserved. Eyes, scales, skeletons were crushed and minced by the teeth of a garbage disposal unit and collected as disgusting mash for use as food by other living beings, because nothing was wasted. The line ended with an aluminum can, oily and sealed. It smelled strongly of fear, urine, fat, adipose wax, blood and rotten marrow.

The silent, gasping bodies of the creatures from the breeding farm were bundled together, waiting, on the bar where they were hanging from big, rusty uncinated hooks, below them, a pool of blood and yellowish matter formed. Every now and then, a white suit approached, removed a specimen from the hook and carried it to the battered conveyor belt covered with scales, clotted liquid and unidentified body parts. For a wild moment, I thought about my mother at the dinner table, harpooning dribbling meat with a fork, about the hungry gaze of my siblings ogling the oil overflowing from the can, about those who had threatened to strike for a raise in salary, those who couldn't cope with it anymore , or those who had seen too much.

Soon I was turned over and grabbed under my armpits by my conveyer, I resumed my train of prayers. My voice was raucous, hoarse from the very little use and too much screaming. I firstly perceived emptiness and void under my feet and I was certain I would have fallen, then the rusty hook plunging in the skin of my back and the unpleasant sensation of gravity, of my whole body spasmodically pulling down and being suspended with resolution, with the sole hold of my living flesh.

I yelled at the top of my voice and my scream was lost in the buzzing of the drills, in the suffering cracking of broken bones, the lacerating noise of ripped flesh, in the shuffling steps of the suits, in the motor turning the rollers of the assembly line pushing the belt to its final destination before abandoning its load and being swallowed by the rotor to start the cycle again. The involuntary swaying of a body made me turn, and I found myself face to face with the girl I had stared at for so long in the water. I didn't feel the breath exhaling from her gasping 'O', maybe she was slowly suffocating. Her entire body was slightly quivering, like that of shellfish in the seafood shop window. Not a feature had changed on that desperate face, the terrified expression was perfectly identical to the one she had in the pen. I couldn't read on it any gleam of will or resignation, just pure, utter horror. I looked closely at her for a few more seconds, before she was chosen from the bunch hanging from the hooks and taken away.

Her eyes were still staring into mine, when the suit placed her on the conveyer belt, grabbed the axe and in one, swift motion took off her head with a neat, clean cut.

# CLOSE YOUR EYES

I was surrounded by a landscape of sleeping pills. People had abandoned themselves on the seats, some bent, with dangling arms brushing the grimy ground; others were sitting upright, hands clutching their chests, or their belongings laid in their laps. The whole thing was a hecatomb of jackets and purses, dozens of them, everywhere. The giant snake of a train ran on, limitless and all the same, chock full of sleeping people. Actually, it was not too surprising. It was early in the morning. But it was still quite shocking to notice that none, really none, were awake or showing the smallest sign of life, not even involuntary, at my passage. Coach after coach, I ran into the same scenario. All there, unconscious, with flaccid puppet limbs, they looked like defenceless larvae. By then, I had gone through five cars, and the string seemed destined to be endlessly repeated, when at last my peripheral vision registered a movement.

Through the glass door, I saw a couple of men in train conductor uniforms looming over a passenger who was resting in an unnatural position. A hand grabbed my arm, making my blood run cold. To my left, down in the gap between two seats, a young guy with wide, fluttering eyes was crouched.

"What are you doing awake?" he whispered nervously, he didn't miss the glance I automatically shot towards the next coach. "Are *they* here?"

I nodded, not really understanding.

"We need to move," he firmly asserted.

He wriggled out of his hiding place and took me by the hand, leading me back, to the car I had just left. When we crossed over, he let go of me and kept on going, swiftly. I felt obliged to follow him.

"We must hide," he declared, hitting the limp head of a man sticking out on an armrest as he passed by. The head did not dangle.

"Do you always take this train?"

I was panting trying to keep up with his pace. The monitor located in the front section of the car had the hour frozen on a pixelated picture, which dated back to the previous day. The ghoulish white light of a milky, dirty sun penetrated through the windows.

"In here?" I asked, pointing at the half-closed door of the toilet.

"They open all the doors. Come on," my companion briskly replied.

He chose a compartment that seemed to me identical to the others, then he grabbed a few jackets and some backpacks. He hinted at me to get down in the gap between two rows of seats. It looked narrow, I thought I would never fit. I balled up in a fetal position. The floor of the train was filthy, and I leaned my face to it. The guy recommended that I stay very still, while he artfully placed some bags to conceal parts of my body that by chance stood out, and then he disappeared. I heard him rummaging around, sound of a zipper, then nothing. For the longest time I laid there. From the crack between the seat and the floor, I could see a man of about thirty, dark beard and hair, with his head tilted to one side. An earplug had fallen from his ear and was sadly dangling a few inches away from his hand, that was still clutching his phone. I could see the limbs of the passenger next to him, and from that angle they looked detached, disconnected from a bust, autonomous life-forms.

The coach door was slammed opened. In the gangway, the joints of the train horribly sizzled one over the other as if they were frying, the noise hurt my ears. The floor under my cheek vibrated with each step, I swallowed dirt and dust at every vibration. Then, my view was obscured for a moment, by the black fabric of one of the conductor's trousers. They were towering over my bunch of seats; I could almost feel their breath. Then, the fabric moved on. The two were silently examining the man in my line of sight with the behavior of surgeons inspecting a patient's belly. A gloved hand rolled the man's head forward, so that it fell on his chest. The pause that followed was surreal, almost suspended. Then, from the hand of the conductor on the right, a nasty-looking gizmo sprouted from nowhere, and it was brought near the passenger's shoulder. It took me a few instants to understand what was going on. The man started to jump like a marionette, tottering over the bodies that sat around him in some sort of spastic ballet, as if someone had pushed the fast-forward button, until he tipped over and fell to the floor with a thud, dropping right in front of me with his dull mask. In falling he had opened his eyes, which were vitreous and light blue. His expression was stuck in a grimace of dumb joy, face crisscrossed by the subtle contraction caused by the electrical shock. The air filled with a sharp smell that made my eyes water. I heard the door opening and closing again. At once, the mask disappeared from my vision field. The body was dragged away, with a nauseatingly slippery noise, then the car door slid closed.

All of a sudden, the bags covering me were ripped off.

"What did you take?" the guy snapped, reaching out to help me up.

"What?" I croaked.

"Why aren't you sleeping? What did you take?" he questioned me again.

I was feeling confused.

"Those men, with their thingamabob, what are they doing?"

"Those are the conductors. They are verifying expiration dates."

"The what?"

I realised my back was damp with a thin layer of cold sweat. He shook his head unhappily.

"I'm not surprised you don't know anything about it; and still, I wonder why it never came to anybody's mind. Nobody thinks about it. About productivity, I mean. Each one of us has a cut-off point. And it's marked exactly..." He ungraciously grabbed the head of a bald man with glasses and turned it forward. The lenses slipped to the ground. Minuscule numbers followed by a seal were impressed on the skin on the back of the man's neck, where the roots of his hair once were. "...here."

"Jesus," I groaned, rubbing the same spot at the nape of my neck with my hand in a reflex action. "I never realised it."

"It's not an easy area to spot," the guy comforted me, "even if you knew it, you would have needed two mirrors with a zoom. Or someone who could read it for you."

We both know that people didn't live with each other anymore, not since a long time ago.

"So that man before, he was..."

"Expired, yeah." he concluded. "Finished, kaput. And as you noticed for yourself, he was quite young. It's personal. It doesn't depend on your age."

He fell silent for a moment, then he offered: "The expired are taken away by the on-board cleaning service."

I stayed silent. I didn't ask myself questions about the man's fate. It was rather predictable what they would have done with an expired product.

"What I don't get," he insisted, "is the reason why you're still awake."

"Why are you? Maybe I'm like you."

"That's impossible" he said, "I'm flawed."

He showed me the back of his neck. On his ebony skin, vague numbers were branded in angry, red marks.

"All of my family was, actually. My parents were, and my sisters as well. I am the last one that - "

He stopped. I looked at the ground. The lenses of the bald man's glasses were cracked.

"Every morning I hide during their shift, it's the only part of the day in which they make their rounds. If you were flawed and unaware of it, they would have macerated you immediately. Then why?" He danced around me as if he was studying a rare beast. "May I?"

The touch of his fingers, as light as it was, burned, like fire. He looked back at me with a flaring gaze.

"You're blurred!" His expression was indecipherable, savage. "Your expiration date has faded, that's why it's the first time this has happened to you."

"Why do you keep showing up at work?"

"What else should I do? Should I miss the morning roll call, then they would know something's wrong. They'd track down my fire and they'd hunt me." He had a point. He shot me a look I recognised as accusing, "And now you, too."

"Me?" I felt frozen. "I don't want to have anything to do with this stuff. I'll go straight to those conductors. I'll explain the situation to them, and I am sure they'll find a solution to -"

The guy grabbed me by the shoulders, and shook me so hard, he made my head spin.

"Don't you understand?" he hissed loudly. "They don't need to fix you, you're just trash, now!"

Panic-stricken, I spit venom.

"I am not like you. This is just a huge misunderstanding. If they want to retype the date, I -"

"But why should you want that?" His eyes were eaten by the fire of a consumed soul. "Why would you want to sit back and close your eyes, now that you know the truth?"

"What's the alternative?" I lost my temper. "To peek every morning from cracks between the seats and spend the rest of my time trying not to show that I'm a defective gear in a perfect machine?"

I stared at his torn and hurt gaze. "I'm sorry. I know you thought you found an accomplice, but it's not me."

I jerked out of his weakened grip.

"Hey! Hey!" I started to shout towards the coach where those leconic public officers disappeared.

At that moment he began to fight. He tried to shut my mouth, and I sank my teeth into the back of his hand. He backed off with a grunt of pain. His hand was bleeding.

"Fuck it," he growled with bulging eyes and ran from the compartment. I was astonished that, instead of aiming for the direction opposite to one the conductors took, he threw himself into the next coach. That would have put him in their laps.

Left alone, I tried to calm down, but I was in shock. I let a few seconds pass, and then I slowly followed him. The lights in the car flickered for a moment, while the train entered a tunnel. The compartment welcomed me in total silence. There was no trace of the Flawed Guy, but on the other end of the coach stood the two conductors, statuesque and sinister, as if they had emerged from nowhere. They showed no sign that they had seen me. They were both looking in the direction of a girl, who sat in the middle of the compartment. She was bent forward, her head resting on the spread legs of a man wearing a hat and a turquoise scarf who was sleeping on the seat in front of her, her blonde hair spread on his belly. The back of her neck was on display, but the expiration date had been replaced by a black, gory clot. Blood was dripping in rivulets down her neck. The conductors looked at each other without a word, one of them pulled out their taser. The girl crackled like popcorn. She slid to the floor with an expression of idiotic beatitude.

The conductor with the taser turned his head in my direction.

At that very moment, a rainfall of suitcases knocked over the two conductors, burying them. The Flawed Guy, perched in the luggage rack, had forcefully kicked them, and now he swooped down as well, in a mayhem of fists and kicks. He was shouting at me to run at the top of his lungs.

I about-faced. Lights came and went, whirling like mad moths. The compartment door didn't open, I hit it head on. I hastily ran back an undefined number of coaches, stumbling on stuff and people. Eventually, I stopped in the space between two cars, to shed the horrible lead feeling that fills your body when you realise everything's lost. The train rumbled on its way, unperturbed, with a hellish, metallic uproar. For the second time, I felt someone's grip grasping me, like a steel trap. I found myself in the Flawed guys arms. I felt the rough fabric of his jacket rub against my face.

"That girl -"

"I'm sorry, but it was the only way to make you believe," he replied, voice muffled by my hair. "Do you understand, now? Not that it matters, anyway." He bitterly added, "They'll search through every nook and cranny of every car. They're after us."

"No. We can't get caught. We need to get off."

Presumably, the doors would have opened for only one stop, the last one. The end of the line, where the Flawed for years had mingled with the crowd of workers who were reawakened numb and, in stretching, complained about their aching backs and bones, blaming their discomfort on the coach seats.

"We need to find a way to go beyond the train!"

"Beyond the train there's only the train," The Flawed replied with a painful smile.

I squeezed him hard by the shoulders.

"We need to find a way."

The next coach was warm with the oblivious collapsed bodies. The Flawed piled several individuals up against the door to block entry.

I had taken the little emergency hammer from the wall and was pitilessly attacking the window with the strength of despair. The cursed glass wouldn't break. What broke was the glass door between the compartments, showering the Flawed in a cascade of splinters. From the wound in the door clawed hands jutted out, and started blindly fishing around, with the intent to scratch and injure, trying to grab, to catch hold.

I was about to inflict a particularly hard blow, when the train shook with an abrupt, fatal jolt. The Flawed hung on, crouched by the door, but I lost my balance, and smacked into an old man sleeping with his hands on his stomach. The hammer flew to the other side of the car. The train entered another tunnel.

The coach precipitated into darkness which was lacerated by the piercing scream of the Flawed, and when the lights came on again, a hand had grabbed him by the hair, and was pulling him upwards with a violent, but steady calmness. Blinded by pain, the Flawed kept on spurring me on, shouting, the train jumped like a pinball machine, turning against us, it was our enemy. I grabbed the hammer and smashed it with all my might down onto the hand scalping the Flawed. The blow scored a hit with a satisfying, sinister noise, and the hand pulled back. With a roar, I threw myself at the window, that exploded in a myriad of shards as sharp as blades, cutting my skin, doodling red streaks on every inch of it.

I stretched my bleeding hand in front of me, and suddenly, I was painlessly deprived of it. It was as if it had been deleted. A crisp, empty darkness was spread in front of me, too deep to be a tunnel. It was a black sheet in which nothing was reflected. A black sheet in which I could dip parts of my body just to witness them disappearing. Absence of matter in time and space. It's hard to explain with words that which does not exist.

It was then that I realised that life beyond that train simply didn't exist, that a life beyond that train hadn't been conceived at all. That leaving the train by willpower or casualty was the same as perishing.

*Beyond the train there's only the train.*

I turned towards the Flawed. A multitude of slimy arms, like viscid tentacles, surrounded him. The compartment door seemed to swell from the force of pressure, and the hinges were on the verge of exploding. Two thumbs were digging black pain into his eye sockets.

I closed my eyes, letting the dark swallow every image, my gaping mouth, like an endless tunnel, incapable of emitting sound, sucking in every scream.

# LAST EPISODE

A man wearing a hat and a turquoise scarf stumbled in the vicinity of a sticky river.

He was exhausted by all that he had witnessed and felt the need to rest a little.

A subtle pollution, worse because it was invisible, had faded the contours of things in its moist fatal mist, and his own outline was now blurred. A breeze which brought no relief whirled at his feet sales receipts, and lottery tickets already scratched-off. Water frothed, but it was a chemical foam. The yellowish sky was silent and suspended. He was now panting. Maybe he should have waited all night for some distant star, which would bring with it the promise of escape, but the night sky was brightly lit, bombed by satellites and drones.

He felt like an enormous sack, empty and flaccid, a wineskin now deformed by all it had been filled with, and therefore unable to go back to its original shape. He felt more of a burden than ever, empty yet heavy. He wanted to take up as little space as possible. He wanted to tiptoe and go unnoticed, be left in peace. Yet reality refused to leave him alone, it struck him, hit him physically with her concrete, unleashed violence.

It all started when the maps began to fill up, not even a blank space left to dream. It followed when the oceans and air were divided into slices, into portions to be savoured by buyers, when outer space was dissected, claimed, grabbed from far away. It faded when paths were dug inside heads that once hosted thoughts too big for skulls so small, when minds were kept occupied to prevent them from lingering on idle and sublime ideas.

He called them the leaking thoughts. He was continuously forced to kick out external intruders from his insides. He was by then capable of recognising an induced thought from an internal one. The leaking ones, that made their way into his head using the nooks in his skull to hide in, profiting from the soft, spongy part of the brain which they consumed, imbibed, they were always colourful, in lighter or darker tones (it depended on the nature of the thought, and on what flaw or desire the mind's possessor needed to focus on, to later find a purchasable remedy), bigger, presenting themselves in rubbery capital letters and tending to take up all the space, to nest.

Floating had been easier, before.

Now, he was a heavy sack of skin, it was his skin that weighed, his skin and bones and bowels, the joints that kept him alive. Alive, not functional – he kept on wandering because he had no function, no place, no purpose. And he would have been perfectly content to solely have the purpose of wandering, if only the act of wandering itself wouldn't have ceased to bring him joy, if only the surroundings didn't smell so much like sharp sulk and despair.

He had been trying to defend himself. To find a shelter in the velvety comfort of the leaf of a plant, so pleasant to rub your finger along; in the transparent shell of the exoskeleton of an insect dragged along by ants, in the joy of a hole in the mesh of a net. In exercising thoughts, astounding ideas... and this suffering, ravenous searching for something never to be found, so well hidden (maybe?) to seem non-existent. And it was so easy, in this laboured, desperate hunt, to get lost. In a rock ripped from the sidewalk, in an overflowing sewer. In the pitiful old scarf lost down the gutter – and all life bursting in. There, in the act of walking with the sole purpose of walking, he had tried to escape from his condition. But more than ever he was dragged away, more often he was pulled away from losing himself, his wandering suspiciously looked upon. Not having a goal to reach was now equivalent to pleading guilty. He was out of time, and because of that he had no time. His time had expired so long ago. There was nowhere to go, in space and time.

The man raised his gaze to the dull sun above, breathing a mouthful of fine particles. And then suddenly he was hit by a renewed sense of awareness – a powerful feeling that left him for a moment even emptier, as if someone had carved into his bowels with a scalpel.

He stretched out his arms, embracing all his surroundings, the soapy river, the burnt weed on the side of the road, the drainage canals choked with trash.

He stretched them out wide, accepting the sky, the ground, the blurry horizon, letting the world slip into his embrace. His heart was beating regularly. He was in touch with it, with his lungs, with his guts.

He looked around, at the burnt weed, the boiling concrete, the oily, greenish water, the fields crammed with agonising insects, and further, to the silent, crumbled mountains. And in between, the pride of the urban cluster, with its regurgitating alleys, big constructions, palaces, shops, schoolhouses, towers pierced with parabolic antennas, and all the lights in the offices, the abandoned buildings left to rot, the ones inhabited by good persons, all the places where the astonishing tragedy of human life was being consumed.

He looked at it all, and, for once, he felt no dismay.

"You win," he said.

He crouched on the sludgy shore, and, looking at himself in the water, reflected.